THE TENANT

And Other Stories

Denys Val Baker

WILLIAM KIMBER · LONDON

First published in 1985 by
WILLIAM KIMBER & CO. LIMITED
100 Jermyn Street, London SW1Y 6EE

© Jess Val Baker, 1985

ISBN 0 7183 0575 2

Photoset in North Wales by
Derek Doyle & Associates Mold, Clwyd
and printed in Great Britain by
Biddles Limited, Guildford, Surrey

Contents

I

The Tenant

Laurie Maxton knew at once when the big bumptious lodger had packed and gone, leaving June Winters and her children to fend for themselves in the basement flat.

It was nothing said or described: just a feeling in the air. He came back from work that evening, letting himself in with his front door key, and in the moment while he walked down the long corridor towards their sitting room he felt the difference. There was an unfamiliar silence emanating from below; perhaps he had become so much in tune with that hidden world that he could not help detecting the change.

He hesitated, and then went into the sitting room. His wife Pam was reading by the fire. She looked up with pleasure and he went across quickly and kissed her. Their kiss was soft and warm, the kiss of a couple happily married for ten years but still delightfully aware of each other.

'Had a good day?' she said.

'So-so.' He paused. 'Any news here?'

She shook her head.

'Children all right?' he persisted.

'Yes. They've had their tea and gone round to play at Sally's. They'll be back soon.'

It wasn't what he wanted. Despite himself, he said:

'How's June?'

His wife smiled. He and the woman in the basement had grown friendly, the more so as the hectoring, overbearing husband and his sweet, rather quiet wife grew estranged.

'She's all right. We went shopping this afternoon.'

Laurie looked at his wife carefully. He wondered that she did not sense any of the feelings which seemed to hover around; as if the very air was loaded with implications and events.

'And Hugo?'

'I expect he'll be back soon – worse luck.'

But he wouldn't. Somehow Laurie knew that – and he knew it for certain a little later, when he went down the winding basement staircase to borrow some sugar.

June Winters was sitting at the small kitchen table, peeling some potatoes. He stood at the doorway watching her, as he had so often stood before. Her movements were slow, precise, regular, as if carried on independently of her mind. She stared, he guessed, not at the potatoes, but through and beyond them into some dreamy world of her own.

He stood, frowning at the realisation of how this irritated him, of how his curiosity about this woman seemed to feed on itself, always growing stronger and stronger.

He remembered his first sight of her. It had been nearly a year ago. He and Pam had decided to let off the basement, and advertised it as a flat in the local paper. The first person to call had been Hugo Winters: big, bouncy confident – he swept into the house, oozing charm and confidence, and before they could say much had declared he would take the flat, but he would just like to bring his wife to see it.

Later that evening Laurie had opened the door in response to the already familiar brusque ringing, and discerned, almost hidden behind the voluble husband, the dim shape of Mrs Winters. She was very much a June: dark, mysteriously smiling, a woman in her early thirties with a large, well formed almost mongolian face set in curious repose so that it presented an almost baffling madonna-like expression. There was, indeed, almost a foreign touch about her; the dark, slightly passé beauty almost Eastern in its secretiveness, its hint of something beyond.

Hugo Winters had once again swept in and somehow, almost as an afterthought, propelled his wife along with him. From the beginning, their relationship seemed to Laurie quite unreal. That they had ever been attracted to one another, lived together, begot two children, all seemed quite unbelievable. They were complete opposites; perhaps the only explanation of their coming together.

At first Laurie had assumed that the woman's withdrawal into herself was a protection against the brash jollity of her husband, the only way in which she was able to endure his company. But gradually, after the family had moved in and he had seen something more of them as an entity, he had realised, to his secret annoyance, that June Winters, if not precisely in love with her husband, was still somehow in his power.

Laurie found himself wondering about this. He would watch Hugo going off each morning to the architect's office where he worked: big, burly, flashily dressed, twirling a tipped cane he always carried, looking quite the man of the world. What on earth could a woman like June see in a man like that?

Sometimes he discussed the problem with Pam. At such times he was able to persuade himself comfortably that it was merely just such a discussion as they might have about several of their friends, quite impersonal and detached.

But sometimes, on his own, in the quiet truth of late night as he went round locking up the house, as he paused for a moment by the door leading downstairs to the basement, hearing the murmur of voices, and wondering what went on down there in that hidden world – at such times he admitted to himself a certain peculiarity about his interest. It had grown up almost unnoticed, built out of momentary contacts – a time when he met June Winters in the high street, struggling with a pram and a small boy and some parcels, and helped her home; a time when the boy had cut himself in the garden, and Laurie went out and took him off to bathe the cut. He was sitting rocking the boy into quiet when he became aware of June Winters standing very close behind him, watching with large eyes that for a moment, he fancied, almost revealed something.

'But what on earth does she see in the man?' he said irritably, after such an encounter. 'He's vulgar and conceited and – and –'

Pam would laugh, and ruffle his hair.

'Maybe he's just her type?'

It was only with a great effort that he would restrain himself from the revealing outburst: 'But he's NOT her type, not her type at all.'

Even so, Laurie began to realise that his interest was becoming an obsession. He talked less and less about the basement and its affairs. Yet, though he talked less, he thought more. When he was at work in the city, supposedly struggling with figures and accounts, he found himself instead struggling with images of June Winters. Her cool, calm, inscrutable face would appear like a shadow across his ledgers. At home, in reality, he doubted if she had ever looked at him full in the eye, it was as if she was in some way frightened to do so. But here, in this dream world, her great eyes seemed to stare at him, almost beseechingly. Help me, he thought they said, rescue me, let me escape from my bondage. Did he imagine it all, or was that really how she felt?

Sometimes he would shake his head as if to shake away the image; telling himself that he must be mad, he was a happily married man with a lovely wife, a nice home, a good job, children, everything running smoothly. What was the point of brooding over a strange woman in the basement, even if she was unhappily married!

But that was the strange thing. He knew of her unhappiness as if by instinct. It was almost as if he had known her before, sometime. He knew by the way she wheeled the pram down the road whether she felt happy or unhappy; he could tell from the tone of her voice everything her words were designed to hide. And there were times when she passed close to him in the passage when he could have sworn that her body moved towards him, just as his arms might suddenly ache to hold her.

'I must be mad, quite mad,' Laurie would tell himself, and banish the image and the thoughts for a while. And then he would come home, and see something, hear something, imagine something; and all his resolutions would be of no avail, a part of him at least would think only about the woman in the basement.

Like tonight ...

'Hullo,' he said from the doorway.

She went on peeling the potatoes, and he realised she had known of his presence all the time. He came into the room uncertainly. The baby lay in the cot in the corner; the little boy would be asleep in the small room next door.

'I came to borrow some sugar.' He went over to the cot, and rocked it thoughtfully.

'What will you do, I mean now ...' He trailed off into silence.

'Is Hugo about?' he said at last, awkwardly.

June Winters put down the knife carefully. She shrugged, as if returning to her present world.

'No, Hugo's not in.'

From the other side of the table Laurie looked down at her steadily. The absence of Hugo, an absence he knew to be real and final, freed him of a strange weight. He felt able to exert the pressure of his personality; he willed her to look up, noting with pleasure the faint flush that coloured the skin of her neck and rose sweetly into her cheeks.

'Yes?' he said softly.

She looked up. She had large, expressive eyes that now were slightly clouded, yet met his gaze. As they did so – perhaps the first time they had ever exchanged such a full glance – Laurie felt a strange tremor run through his body.

'He's gone, hasn't he?'

June Winters lowered her eyes, picked up the knife and started peeling the potatoes again.

Laurie watched, curiously content. He felt he could have stood watching this woman endlessly, the slow, graceful movement of her neck, the oriental timelessness of her image. What was it that drew him like this – what made both of them feel like this? For feel they both did, he knew: it was in the air all the time, slumbering perhaps, but there: and both of them indulged secretly in acknowledging it, far beneath the surface.

Nothing further was said about Hugo. Laurie took the sugar upstairs, and he and Pam spent the evening watching television. The next day he went off to work, and in the evening Pam met him and they went out for a meal. Life went on its normal course and he hardly saw June Winters until a week later, when she called out to say that her lights had fused. He went down with a torch and some wire.

'Hullo,' he said cheerfully, flashing the torch around.

She was standing by the fuse box, the baby in her arms, and the little boy clutching at her legs. There was something curiously poignant in the picture. Quickly Laurie moved the torchlight on to the box and began searching for the blown fuse.

When he had mended it and the lights came on again, the entire basement was almost dazzlingly floodlit. It was as if some external force was determined ruthlessly to expose June Winters' privacy. It was impossible for Laurie not to look quickly around, through the open door into the bedroom, into the small lounge. Everywhere there was a pointed absence of the usual signs of male occupation: there was no Hugo's hat, no Hugo's coat, no Hugo's clothes – no Hugo.

She had gone to sit in an armchair by the fire. Her head was inclined downwards. She played absent-mindedly with the baby, now lying on the hearth.

Laurie stood uncertainly in the centre of the room. All at once, almost without thinking, he began talking. He found himself telling the quiet woman opposite all about his day at the office, the things he had heard, what he saw on the way home ... And curiously, in some subterranean way, he broke through her reserve, so that she began talking back, almost animatedly. Soon they were discussing, debating, even arguing, in the way that any couple might do. Laurie found this strangely pleasing, an intimacy he had imagined but which had not before been expressed. Before they finished talking he and June Winters were laughing out aloud.

'Ah, well, I must go now,' he said, remembering Pam, upstairs. 'I'm – glad I was able to mend the fuse.'

'So am I.' She looked quickly at Laurie, and he could have sworn that for the moment the veil lifted, the eyes were clear and compelling in their message.

'It's nice to know there's a man about the house, now I'm on my own.'

He moved to the door, uncertain what to say now that the position had been admitted. At the door he turned. She had risen to reach for something from the cupboard. At his movement she paused and looked sideways at him, her body poised in a curving, vibrant arch. In the firelight her figure was outlined softly, made to seem aglow with hidden life.

She did not move, though he knew she was aware of his glance. She smiled faintly, looking across at him: and in his heart Laurie knew he had reached the point of no return.

'Goodnight, then,' he said, almost gruffly, and went upstairs.

It wasn't quite as he had expected. When he was back with his wife, sitting by the familiar fire, doing the familiar things, he found it hard to believe that he had participated in the events downstairs. In some way it was as if, among all the babel of conversation, he and the woman had faced up to their situation. The truth was now exposed. All right, June Winters had said, I know you have secretly been drawn to me for a long time – now I am all alone, and what do you want to do about it?

Curiously, Laurie found himself avoiding the issue. Perhaps he was rather like a man on a swing, or attached to some curious elastic rope that swung first in one direction, then in the next. All at once he became almost painfully conscious of his wife, Pam. They had been married for ten years, and each year they had drawn closer together. Their tastes, their interests, even their habits, were curiously alike. They had developed a mutual fondness and understanding, as well as a passionate love for one another. How then could he feel in any way for another woman?

He had asked himself the question before, of course. But now he asked the question, without bothering to answer it, as a shield to protect himself and his marriage. How indeed could he imagine looking at another woman? Even if his motives were mixed, he felt himself drawn again to his wife, remembering the long woven tapestry of their marriage: and somehow he managed to avoid going down to the basement, into the secret waiting world of June Winters.

Life seemed to go on, week after week. June Winters put her children into a nursery and took a part-time job. By mutual consent Laurie and Pam reduced her rent by a pound, so that with what she earned she was able to manage. Of Hugo there was no further news; he had just disappeared completely.

And then one morning, Pam had a telephone call to say that her mother was ill. It was one of those emergencies about which there can be no argument. Laurie put her and the children on the mid-day train and kissed her an uneasy goodbye. Then he went off into town for lunch, and afterwards stayed late working at the office.

It was about eight o'clock when he got back to the house. It was strange to find it in darkness: though there was a bright light from the basement. He went into the front room and switched the light on, grimacing at the cold emptiness of a room uninhabited. He went through to the kitchen and lit the stove to make a cup of tea.

For a time he pottered about, rather morosely. When the tea was made he took it into the front room and sat down at the table. He looked at his watch: it was half past eight. The evening stretched before him interminably, tantalisingly. Below, he was aware of June Winters, moving softly about her domain, backwards and forwards. He imagined her feeding the baby, tucking up the little boy, returning to her room. He thought of her sitting there, perhaps reading a book, perhaps ...

He went to the top of the basement, and called out.

'June? June, are you in?'

There was no answer. Yet he knew she must be there. Almost without thinking he descended the steps quietly, one by one. At the bottom he paused, and tapped on the kitchen door. Then he went in.

She was sitting at the table, alone. It was almost as if he had never left the room, as if it was still that earlier evening when he had stood by the door and looked across at her, with her body curved, her head held forward, her hair falling down in cascades of dark oblivion.

'Ah,' he said. 'Hullo ...'

Was it his imagination, did she incline her head, silently. Puzzled, he stood there; uncertainly he made a half movement. Then he paused, aware suddenly of the tension. All at once the knowledge flooded through him: she's been sitting here, waiting, all the time – she came home and put the children to bed, she performed all the customary actions, but all the time, like me upstairs, she's been waiting and wondering, waiting and wondering ...

He eyed her with a sudden tenderness. Somehow the knowledge seemed to bind them closer in their curious, secret mesh of understanding. Almost without being aware of it, he began to speak to her.

'Do you know the first time I ever saw you? Hugo came to the door and you were there over his shoulder, over his big, ugly shoulder. You just looked from behind him with those big eyes of yours and I thought you were something beautiful and unreal. I wanted to open my arms to you ... I can't

understand, you and Hugo ... why you married. I often sit and
look out of a window and wonder about those things.'

He paused, his voice muffled, and in the silence he was
aware of his own beating heart.

'June ...'

Suddenly he saw her hands on the table in front of her. They
were gripping the table hard, fiercely; he could see the whites
of the knuckles. He realised in that moment that she was
holding herself there, willing him to go away – yet somehow
she could not speak the words. He hesitated, wondering if he
could bring himself to turn and go up the stairs to the barren
rooms above; knowing he couldn't.

'June ...' he said, helplessly.

He half moved into the room, and at the same moment she
jumped up and ran into his arms, and he was holding her
tight, close to his breast, that dark hair, as he had often
imagined it, nestling against his cheek, the sound of her fast
beating heart thumping against his own. He held her like that
for some time, and then she raised her face, with her eyes
closed and lips opening to meet his in a kiss that was yearning
and passionate, and yet somehow tinged with sadness. Looking
back afterwards he often thought that the whole of their
strange relationship was encompassed in that kiss, that
embrace. It was as if all those evening encounters, those secret
glances, those moments, had built up to this one, final,
enduring moment.

'Do you know –' he tilted up her chin, so that he could look
into her eyes '– how often I've wanted to do that?'

She nodded.

'And you?' he asked, tentatively.

She nodded again, and he felt her arms creep around him.

'I love you,' she whispered.

He looked at her wondering: seeing in that moment, as if
mirrored in her eyes, a clear portrait of someone else, his own
wife, Pam. How was it possible? Yet ...

'And I love you.'

It was true, wasn't it? For there was now nothing but truth
between them. Everything that had happened, and that would
somehow never happen, was something they shared through
this strange feeling of lovingness. In life, he thought with

sudden understanding, there is an infinity of space for love.

'Supposing ...' she was speaking now, her voice low and wistful. 'Supposing we had met another time, another life.'

'Another life,' he echoed; and holding her in his arms, so strange and yet so familiar, he became almost physically and painfully aware of that other life. 'Would we have recognised each other?'

'Yes,' she said confidently.

With one finger he traced the outline of her nose, the way the tip turned up.

'I would have recognised this, perhaps,' he said teasingly.

Their laughter was uneasy, as if likely at any moment to turn into tears. Laurie eased his back against the wall and looked down, raising his hand to stroke the long dark hair.

'I often used to imagine this, stroking your hair, holding you, just quietly, like this.'

'I know.'

With some difficulty he pronounced the words which somehow he knew would break the strange spell.

'What will you do? I mean ... if Hugo's gone ...'

As he spoke, involuntarily his arms tightened around her, and for a moment they could not speak any more, clinging to each other helplessly. When, unwillingly, he slackened his grasp, she looked up at him with large and luminous eyes, looking in some way more beautiful than he had ever seen before. Staring into their mysterious depths he was aware of how easily he could drown in their sea – and yet how important it was for both of them that he should not.

'I was going to tell you – and Pam –' She broke the silence almost harshly. 'But I couldn't bring myself to before –' She made a gesture, and smiled. 'Somehow, now, it makes it easier ...'

'You mean,' he said quickly, ardently, 'now that we've said what we always felt?'

She nodded.

'I – I've decided to leave. I have a sister living down in Cornwall. I can share her house, get the children into a school and take a job. Perhaps pottery – I used to be a student once.'

'When will you go?'

'Soon ... in a week.'

'A week!' He hesitated, looking at her: and both knew what was in that look. A week – perhaps in a week they could snatch at their happiness, perhaps in a few days they could miraculously grasp the wonder which both felt might lie waiting for them, somewhere. Perhaps they could defy and defeat all the forces arrayed against them?

They knew they couldn't. And in that moment, imperceptibly, they seemed to withdraw from their exposed position, from the brink of the unknown precipice. It was no movement, nothing said; just something felt, sadly and inevitably; and perhaps, curiously, with a certain relief.

'Come,' Laurie said at last, able on a less passionate level to speak more freely. 'Come and sit by your fire, and you can sit with your head on my lap and we can talk and talk …'

They went over to the fire, and Laurie picked up the poker and stirred the sullen coals into a cosy flame. He sat in the chair and June Winters knelt on the floor, resting her dark hair on his lap. There was around them a sudden sense as of peace. It was almost as if their passion had been sublimated by a feeling of rightness; as if perhaps by not grasping greedily at their immediate fulfilment they had in some way enriched their relationship, giving it just that strength which would enable them to bear their separation.

They sat by the fire for a long time. Laurie lost track of time. It did not seem important. He only stirred when at last the fire burned low and their bodies began to shiver with the creeping cold.

He had thought by now she was asleep, but at his movement she turned quickly. Her hand came up and touched his cheek thoughtfully.

'You know,' she said quietly, 'I'm glad – glad it's been like this.'

He nodded, thinking of Pam, glad that he would be able to talk to her one day about this, to explain it to her because it had been preserved as something complete and lovely.

'It's strange,' he began, and stopped.

'Strange – that you love Pam, and yet you love me?' She smiled, with a woman's wisdom. 'I don't suppose your wife will think so, not really. In life nothing is beyond comprehension, anything is possible.'

At her words he paused, and bent forward, cupping her head between his hands. He looked closely into her eyes, knowing that he would never altogether plumb their depths, yet grateful for these moments of understanding, of togetherness.

'I must go now.' He kissed her gently, feeling her lips soft and moist, wistful in their clinging.

'Good night, my love.'

'Good night, darling.'

He went over to the door and then, struck by the remembrance, turned yet again. She sat by the fire, pensively, her head half turned. He felt the need to say something, yet it never could be said. With a faint sigh, he turned and went away up the stairs.

A week later, June Winters went away. It was a cool but clear day, coloured with enough sunshine to hint at the summer days to come.

'You'll love it in Cornwall,' said Pam, standing in the doorway. 'It'll be like a new life.'

June Winters smiled her composed, confident smile. She looked, in her madonna-like way, very cool and lovely.

'That's what I need ... a new life.'

She ushered the children into the waiting taxi, and turned and waved. In a moment or two, she was gone, almost as if she had never really existed.

At first Laurie could not quite accept it. Surreptitiously, during that evening, he went to the top of the stairs, opening the door and peering down at the darkness below. Was it possible that such emptiness had been occupied? – that children had run about, that she had sat there, her head bent low, at the kitchen table?

He shook his head, puzzled; a little hurt, a little sad, and yet perhaps a little relieved. In the end, when he came to shut the door, he felt as if he was closing it on a part of life itself; and yet doors must be closed, to shut out the vagrant winds of memory.

'Pam,' he said thoughtfully, going up to their bedroom, where his wife was sitting at the dressing table in her nightdress, brushing her hair. 'What about the basement?

Shall we let it again, or shall we –'

He paused, staring into the mirror, seeing his wife's reflection. Suddenly she looked back at him as someone young and fresh and lovely, innocent of all the blemishes and shadows that fell around his own image. He felt suddenly humbled at the realisation that she was his wife, that they belonged together, held by some precious bond. A wave of protectiveness swept over him, a warm desire to preserve their long reality.

He bent down and kissed his wife's warm, living shoulder.

'No ... on second thoughts I don't think we'll let the basement after all.'

II

When We Were Young

They met every afternoon at the village cross-roads and then rode their bicycles wildly down the winding lane to the sea, calling out and singing and hooting cheekily at anyone they happened to pass. The bicycles were all part of the gladiatorial procedure, even though they were thrown aside abruptly on reaching the sand-dunes that marked, like crumbling portals the entry to paradise. Sometimes they paused awhile among the dunes, tempted by the hilltops of Arizona to play their fleeting roles of Jessie James and his brothers, or Wild Bill Hickok or Captain Cody ... But it was no more than a passing whim: soon they would be on their way, eager to breast the last barrier between them and the waiting sea, clean and greeny-blue and shimmering in the slanting sunlight.

There were six of them, and Mick was the precarious sixth, taken into the charmed circle for some reason he had long forgotten. That indeed was the marvellous part of it all: once you were there, a part of them, the past did not exist – there was only now. Life had always been like this, a succession of endless periods of wonder, scampering joyfully across warm sands that became your private playground, splashing with abandon in your secret sea; at last striking out powerfully towards a perpetual golden horizon.

They were all good swimmers, but it was more than that. They were *the* swimmers, romantic and renowned. It was something which began with the bicycle ride, that disdainful, heads-in-the-air, reckless journey through the leafy lane – even this curiously communal act at once cut them off from their fellows. They rode along, often all abreast, like some column of majesty bound for great ceremonies. And when they reached the flat white sands of the deserted beach they were as gods entering some ancient kingdom.

Mick was the youngest, Gerry the next youngest: imperceptibly they kept together, a part of, yet slightly protected from, the elder boys. It was a difference of slight degree that each meeting served to diminish – indeed, as if to emphasise their communion with the others, Mick and Gerry would sometimes vie with one another to be first to accomplish some feat, like swimming out to the old wreck and back. When they did this, though, they remained somehow self-conscious, Mick and Gerry, thrashing through the water, arms flailing, legs kicking, still two boys from the local secondary school out for a bit of fun in the sea. But when, suddenly, the others gave warning shouts and came diving in one after another from the big rock and there were not just the two of them but all of them, diving and gliding and slipping through the water like elusive eels – well, then, somehow, everything was different. It was magic and marvel and mystery, all rolled into one.

Mick knew it was like this not through his mind, but in some physical, intuitive way. Sometimes he might stop swimming, tread water for a moment and watch the others swirling around like white ghosts, diving and leaping in bewildering and fantastic sequences ... And then all at once, almost without realising, he would find himself no longer apart, but moving with them again, diving this way and that, at one again with the endless pattern.

They were the swimmers, inhabitants of another planet, of a watery world where the horizons were infinite, the sea their bountiful mother, the sandy bottom their beloved home. They swam together in impeccable unison, from one rocky cove to another, as swift and sure as the silvery fish around them. And sometimes, indeed, in their deep water dreams, it seemed that they had left their outside, mundane world, and were nearer to the fish and the fossils, the plankton and the sea-anemones, than ever they could be to crotchety parents and impatient schoolteachers. They weaved and turned, sometimes disappearing deep under the green-eyed water, other times hurling themselves high into the air ... And when it was all over and they stood on the sands rubbing themselves down with towels and looking around at all their private wonder Mick not only felt but knew they were gods, indeed, at the close of some truly mystic ritual.

*

One afternoon, unexpectedly, the others did not arrive, there
were only Mick and Gerry, leaning uncertainly on their bright
bicycles and scanning the roads in all directions. When they
had waited at least half an hour they gave up hope and looked
at one another, puzzled ... but it was such a lovely afternoon,
the sky blue, the sun warm and friendly, they could hardly
resist the temptaion. As of one mind they jumped on their
bikes and raced away, down the long familiar lane and out
upon the sand-dunes.

Mick was the first in the water, racing down and throwing
himself in a clean crisp dive straight into the heart of an
oncoming wave. As he emerged the other side and turned to
watch the flash of Gerry, diving after him, he was surprised by
an unfamiliar tingle of excitement almost as if a voice was
whispering somewhere inside him: this is a different sort of
time.

He could never be sure afterwards what subterranean
impulse prompted him to suggest to Gerry:

'Let's swim over to the west beach. We don't often go there.'

They did not go there, really, because too often
holidaymakers found their way down to that particular beach,
but at this time of year this was not likely. Swimming
powerfully, they soon rounded the small point and found
themselves being carried gently up on to the white sands.

After lying for a while stretched out in the warmth of the sun
Mick raised himself on one elbow and was about to order the
retreat back into the familiar sea when he gave an exclamation.

Gerry turned round, puzzled.

'What is it? What's the matter?'

Mick pointed. Over by a small rocky cove at one end of the
beach there was a flurry of splashing and spraying out in the
water.

'It could be seals,' said Mick.

'Or maybe a dolphin?' said Gerry.

Without wasting any more words they both dived back into
the sea and swam along the perimeter of the beach until they
were quite close to the movements. It was clearly neither seals

nor a dolphin but two young girls in black swim-suits. One had long blonde hair tied back with a handkerchief: the other was darker, with a mop of curly hair. The two of them were splashing around in the water and playfully teasing one another, but when they caught sight of the two boys they seemed to take fright and with distant giggles swam to the shore. There they climbed up on to a long flat rock and sat close together, surveying the intrusion.

For a while Mick and Gerry swam around rather aimlessly, once or twice diving so as to show off their prowess. At last Mick called out to the girls.

'Aren't you coming in?'

There were more giggles, and shakings of the head.

'Go on,' cried Gerry teasingly. 'Bet you can't really swim!'

This challenge seemed more effective, for suddenly the two girls climbed up on the edge of the rock and poised themselves to dive. Silhouetted against the sunlight their figures become weirdly illuminated: to Mick, watching, it was almost as if they were surrounded by shimmering halos.

When the girls were in the water Mick and Gerry swam lazily towards them. Soon the four of them were bobbing around, waiting for someone to break the silence.

'Are you down on holiday?' said Mick at last.

The girl with the fair hair nodded. Now that they were closer Mick saw that she had bright blue eyes, as blue as the sea itself, and a way of looking right through him. He felt himself blushing.

'Where do you come from then?'

The girl named a city so far away that so far as Mick was concerned it might have been in Russia. He gave a soft whistle.

'That's a long way to come.'

Gerry meanwhile having ascertained that the other girl had also come this enormous distance, the conversation hung fire. At last, still feeling unfamiliarly shy, Mick said to the blonde girl.

'What about a race to that rock over there? Gerry and I will give you a start, won't we, Gerry?'

The start was contemptuously refused and the race was therefore something of a procession, but at the end of it they all felt more friendly to one another. The girls complimented

Mick and Gerry on their crawl stroke and the two boys said the girls weren't so bad themselves. Actually Mick thought, privately, that the blonde girl was a better swimmer than her friend and he tried, when they were a little apart from the others, to tell her so.

'I don't think I am, not really,' said the blonde girl.

'Yes you are,' protested Mick. 'I watched the way you dived in – you were much faster.'

The blonde girl surprised him by laughing out aloud. When she did that her bright blue eyes sparkled and she seemed to become much more alive.

'You're a funny boy,' she said.

'Funny, how? Ha-ha, or the other?'

'I meant the other – strange, peculiar.' She looked across to where her friend and Gerry were chattering away. 'Is your friend like that, too?'

Mick looked across at Gerry curiously, seeing him almost for the first time as a separate being.

'I don't know really ...'

Uncertainly he embarked on an attempt to explain their circumstances, finding it more difficult than he might have supposed.

'You see, there's a whole lot of us ... we come out swimming every afternoon, after school ... it's fun, it really is ...'

The blonde girl listened politely, but Mick sensed a failure of communication.

'You know how it is,' he said, a little desperately, 'when there's a gang of you ...'

'What's that rock over there?' said the blonde girl abruptly. 'Can we dive from there?'

Oddly, instead of being annoyed at her interruption Mick found himself assenting eagerly. He led the way, the blonde girl swimming just behind, until they had rounded the small finger of rocks that jutted out.

'Why, look,' said the blonde girl, 'there's another little beach. Let's explore.'

Mick had been to the little beach before and had never felt inclined to explore, but somehow this time he was quite pleased to follow the girl up on to the white, white sands. There they lay for a few moments, letting each gentle wave carry them forward a little further.

'Gosh, I love doing this,' said the blonde girl, instinctively arching her body to ride the next wave.

'Do you?' Mick felt oddly superior. 'You should try proper surfing, like we do sometimes over on the big beach. We don't have a board though, we just wait till we catch a wave before it breaks, and hold ourselves rigid like this ... and then we come zooming in.'

'Gosh,' said the blonde girl, blue eyes widening. 'That must be great.'

Mick looked at her wonderingly, seeing for a moment the girl's fresh brown face, the smiling eyes, the wisps of blonde hair ... and then, guiltily, seeing all around, like accusing ghosts, those other more familiar faces.

'Yes,' he said, awkwardly. 'It's great, just great.'

But then, feeling impelled to drop the subject, he went on hastily:

'Let's go on the rocks.'

When they had climbed up on to the top rock they sat side by side, surveying the scene. Now that they had time to look around Mick realised that Gerry and the other girl had not immediately followed them, as he had imagined. Instead they seemed to be playing some sort of teasing game over by the other rocks, jumping up in the water and then pretending to sink, laughing and shouting.

Uncertain, Mick shot a quick look at the girl beside him and saw that she was watching with amusement, her mouth open and her teeth gleaming and blue eyes sparkling. Relieved, he began laughing himself.

'They're enjoying themselves.'

'Yes,' said the blonde girl. 'Tina likes a bit of fun.'

'Tina?' Mick repeated the name thoughtfully. 'That's a nice name. Here, I say,' he went on boldly. 'What's your name?'

'Oh, mine's very ordinary. It's Jane.' She giggled. 'Plain Jane.'

Mick stood up suddenly and advanced to the edge of the rock.

'It's not ordinary at all, it's very nice,' he said. And then, over his shoulder, just as he dived, 'And you're not plain – you're pretty.'

He hit the water clean as a knife and scythed a long curved passage down and down, seeing with sudden avid interest all the magic around him, the spawning plankton, the darting eels, the silver and reddy gold of other denizens of this wonder world ... Then, strangely dissatisfied with it all, he curved up again and broke surface – just in time to see the marvellous sight of the blonde girl called Jane searing through the sky towards him, arms outstretched, face composed, sweeping like a beautiful golden bird into the polished mirror of the water.

'I thought you were going to hit me,' he said lightly, when Jane came up again, her hair once more wet and long, like a mermaid's. He grinned. 'I wouldn't have minded.'

They swam around and then back to the rock, climbing out of the clinging water with some difficulty. Mick was up first and bent over holding out a hand to Jane, pulling her up with a quick united ripple of movement. They stood for a moment side by side, smiling uncertainly at one another: then, as if two minds with a single thought, turned and ran over to the rock tip.

'One – two – three – go!' called out Mick: and in exciting unison the two of them leapt forward and dived deep into the water.

'Gosh,' exclaimed Jane, when she came up, spluttering. 'That was wonderful ... Let's do it again!'

They dived together again, and again and again, each time somehow a little closer, a little more perfectly, it seemed to Mick. After a while it was so exhilarating that he wondered if perhaps they ought not to call over Gerry and Tina ... he even opened his mouth to make the suggestion, and then somehow, seeing Jane beside him poised for her next dive, her blue eyes staring brightly ahead, her whole being tensed up for the experience to come, he felt unable to speak. Suddenly he found he was not thinking about Gerry and Tina at all: only, in wonder, about how he would rather be standing there with Jane than anywhere else in the whole world.

Later they joined the other two and they all lay on the soft white sands, basking in the early evening sun. There was a kind of perverse laziness over them now, but they managed to sketch in each other's portraits a little further. Jane and Tina were both nearing their last year at grammar school, if they managed to get enough O levels they might try eventually for one of the new universities ... but it all seemed a long way ahead.

'And what will you do, Mick?' asked Jane, turning over on her side and examining him with flattering but embarrassing interest.

'Oh ...' He made a large, rather helpless circle in the sand with his finger, aware as he did so, more vividly than ever before him his life, how little time he had allowed to the future. '... something or other, I expect.'

And even as he spoke the inadequate words he looked at Jane, suffused by strange feelings unknown to him before, a wish to blurt out all kinds of wild crazy remarks. Almost as if perhaps she heard them through the silence Jane suddenly turned and looked at him, and for that moment Mick knew, intuitively, that the look was a very private one, to be remembered and remembered ...

Soon afterwards the girls said they would have to get back to the guest house where they were staying with their families. Mick and Gerry walked with them to the top of their end of the beach, and then stood about awkwardly prolonging the farewell.

'Well,' said Jane. 'We must go.' She hesitated. 'See you tomorrow, perhaps?'

Mick avoided looking at Gerry.

'Yes ... yes, that's right.' He began waving as the girls turned and went over to the road. 'See you tomorrow.'

But tomorrow, he thought, all the way back on the strangely silent journey with Gerry – tomorrow would be a different day: that was the same as every other day.

Sure enough when he and Gerry arrived early at the cross roads and leaned pensively over their silvery bicycle handles, perhaps each thinking traitorous thoughts, they had hardly been waiting five minutes before the others came hurtling up with their separate dust clouds and loud hurrahs and welcomes. And in no time at all the gladiators were riding away again, sweeping down the green lane with wild cries and searing up on to the sand-dunes trailing clouds of golden glory. And almost before he knew it Mick was stripped with the others and running across the sands, hot under his bare feet from the day long sun – and they were diving one after the other into the cool, cool water: the swimmers, the wonder boys, bringing with them their own perpetual amazement, spurting and soaring and weaving and gliding like creatures of the deep. Was it not something miraculous, beyond everything else?

But then, out of the corner of his eye, Mick caught sight of a mermaid sitting on a distant rock, combing her long golden hair like any true mermaid ... and beside him Gerry glimpsed another mermaid, also sunning herself. What a strange and exciting thing it was, thought Mick treading water furiously, to have a mermaid come out of the water from the ends of the earth, and just sit there waiting for you.

Already, guiltily, he and Gerry were swimming away from the endless intricate movements of the others. They swam silently and powerfully, afraid to look back at first, and after that wanting only to look ahead. They swam on and on until they were somehow back in the familiar wonder of yesterday, at the edge of the secret white beach.

Mick swam right to the edge of the rock on which Jane sat, dangling her brown legs.

'Hullo,' he called. 'Hullo, mermaid!'

A moment later the two waiting girls had risen, laughing, and dived in to join the boys; and the four of them were laughing and playing in the water as if they had known each other all their lives. But really, Mick thought, feeling immensely older and wiser, life was only just beginning.

III

Miss Meakin's Burglar

Miss Meakin was, as her name suggested, one of those whom the scriptures ordain shall inherit the earth yet persistently efface themselves before such a prospect; a small, tidy woman in her early forties, soberly dressed, well-washed, pink-faced, grey hair wound into a prim bun, pert mouth not quite sure of itself and big brown eyes welling with kind thoughts behind their round, round glasses. She was an only child who had somehow not been shown the door out of the nursery until it was much too late, grown up into a faithful devotee of library books and women's magazines, an earnest patron of Odeon and Regal cinemas, a solitary nibbler of plain-cake teas in Boots' and Lyons' cafés.

When Miss Meakin was twenty-three her mother, a pious if somewhat dominating woman, died of a heart attack (her father had been dead ten years) and she moved from their little house in Ealing to a little bed-sitting-room in Putney. When she was twenty-eight she became a Sunday School teacher at a local non-conformist chapel. When she was thirty-four Messrs. Goodforalls Stores, for whom she had worked ten years, appointed her from the position of third to that of second assistant in the stationery department. When she was thirty-seven she was one of the fourteen occupants of a trolley-bus which skidded and crashed into a public lavatory; her name was in the papers because she bit her tongue in the excitement and was thus classed as slightly injured. When she was forty she moved from her boarding-house in Putney to another boarding-house in Putney. These represented the main events in Miss Meakin's earthly life (pallid, of course, by comparison with the almost daily excitements encountered in books and cinemas). There was no reason why this life should not proceed on its even course. In three or four years' time, for instance, it was extremely probable that she would be made first assistant in the stationery department. But it was not to be quite so. Fate had a little trick to slip into the pack.

One morning Miss Meakin was called upon to serve a young man who required a copy of a *Last Will and Testament*. As he seemed rather young to be needing such a grim document, Miss Meakin could not restrain herself from studying him covertly. He was not the sort of young man of whom she would normally have approved. He wore a flashy pin-striped suit; his collar was dirty and awry, his face unwashed and notable for a stubble of hair; and his hair was far too long and not even brushed back so that it hung tousled and unkempt about his forehead. He also had extremely large ears which stuck out sideways and gave to his face a strange element of foxiness. But there was about his expression such a look of gloominess that Miss Meakin felt quite touched, and as she handed over the will she felt a strong desire to express some words of comfort, such as 'Every cloud has a silver lining, you know, sir.' Being far too shy to step out of her character to that extent she let him go his way uncomforted. But she watched him carefully until he disappeared through the swing-doors into that strange world where he filled up *Last Will and Testament* forms.

She did not, of course, ever expect to see the young man again. That was where Fate played its part. The same lunchtime, it being a sunny day, Miss Meakin took her packet of cheese and watercress sandwiches along to a promenade beside the muddy banks of the River Thames and sat herself primly on one of the iron seats which some long-deceased Parks Superintendent had provided. She opened her library book and opened her packet of sandwiches, years of habit having combined the two actions almost into one, and began to devour them. But after a while she felt uncomfortable, aware of a strange sensation – as if someone else was sharing the taste of her food, if not the tale of her book. Looking up, she was startled to see her neighbour at the other end of the seat leaning towards her, visibly licking his lips. It seemed at the moment rather less startling that it was none other than the young man whom she had served that morning.

'Aaah!' said the young man.

'Is anything the matter?' asked Miss Meakin nervously.

'The matter?' echoed the young man. He seemed to have great difficulty in removing his gaze from the sandwich which

Miss Meakin held in mid-air. 'Oh, no, lady, nothing. Fine day, ain't it?'

'Yes, indeed,' Miss Meakin flustered. 'Yes, indeed,' she repeated being unable to think of anything else to say.

The young man shifted noticeably along the seat and bent towards her in a confiding manner. His eyes were once again trained upon the sandwich. It dawned at last even on Miss Meakin that he looked rather hungry.

'Er – would you – would you like a sandwich?'

The young man looked away.

'Oh, please. I'm not very hungry anyway,' said Miss Meakin, lying valiantly in the best tradition of the many film Samaritans she had observed in the course of her cinema-going.

The young man hesitated.

'Orlright, lady. Many thanks.'

He picked out two sandwiches and munched at them with the desperate relish of one who has, in fact, not eaten for quite a while. He ate clumsily, scattering crumbs down his coat, a mannerism which normally would have affronted Miss Meakin but which now she found herself overlooking, because of her curiosity.

'I remember you,' said the young man gallantly. 'You served me this morning.'

Miss Meakin blushed.

There was a little pause, during which Miss Meakin sensed that she was expected to say something but couldn't think what.

'I do hope you're not in any trouble?' she ventured at last. 'I couldn't help noticing what you bought this morning. I do hope –'

'You've a kind face,' said the young man suddenly.

'Have I?' Taken aback, Miss Meakin realized it was the second compliment she had been paid in a few minutes, but failed to see anything unusual in this.

'You look a good sort. A feller can talk to you.' The young man stretched his hand out for the last sandwich. 'You wouldn't split.'

'Split?'

'I mean,' he cleared his throat noisily. 'I mean, you're the sort of lady what would respect a man's confidings.'

'If I can help in any way, Mr – Mr –'

'Percy's the name. Well, it's like this, lady. It ain't right, now is it, for a fella never to be able to talk to folk – about certain things, I mean.'

'No-o, I suppose not.'

'Sometimes I gets depressed, see, and I feel I want to get a few things off my chest and it's sort of difficult to find someone you can trust. But I guess you won't mind, will you?'

The young man shifted in his seat, making himself more comfortable. His face broke into an unexpected, toothy smile.

'Who'd have thought I'd once been a Boy Scout and gone to Sunday School!'

Miss Meakin, feeling on surer ground, was about to mention her own connection with Sunday Schools when Percy plunged on.

'Mind you, it ain't that I ain't tried. I've not become what I *am* without a struggle, you might say. Oh, no.' He folded his arms, and crossed and uncrossed his legs restlessly, as if his mind was wandering back indignantly to his early struggles to avoid being whatever he now was.

'It began silly like, in a fit of temper. All over my brother Syd and his fur coat.'

'Fur coat?' said Miss Meakin. 'Do men –?'

The young man permitted a half smile to ease the gloomy flatness of his expression.

'It was an ordinary overcoat, lady, but it 'ad a fur-lined collar. My, it was a fine coat, that. Cost 'im about twenty quid, I fancy. Still, Syd allus was lucky at making money ... And I only wanted to borrow it for an evening. Just once. Don't suppose I'd ever have wanted to borrow it again.' He shot Miss Meakin a sudden sly, unabashed look. 'P'raps I would though, eh?' And he chuckled, obviously already in a better humour.

'Anyway, Syd wouldn't lend it me on any account. Mad? Why I nearly went for him there and then. But I didn't. I just stood and told him to take his coat and burn it. Because, I said, *I'm* going out and get meself one *twice* as good.'

Percy's voice warmed at the memory of this verbal onslaught.

'And what happened?' asked Miss Meakin nervously.

'What happened? Why, I goes out and in half an hour I'm back like I said, with a coat twice as good. At least, twice as valuable. Tell you the truth, I still didn't like the look of it as much as Syd's.'

'But where – ?'

'Where did I get it? Pinched it, lady.'

'Oh,' said Miss Meakin in a small voice. 'You mean you – you stole it?'

'That's right. Nipped up the back of Leverson's tailor-shop, climbed the roof and got in through the attic window of his store-room. It was easy.'

Percy eyed Miss Meakin cautiously.

'Haven't shocked you, have I?'

'N-no.'

'Fine,' said Percy, and proceeded to impart one shock after another. 'Well, that's how it began. They never caught me. Why, I did the same place only a week later. That time I was more fly – I took six coats instead of one. Then I had a try at private houses, you know, jewellery and money and so on. 'Course they caught me in the end. It was a job over at New Cross. A gown shop. Supposed to be no one about, but the manager had worked late and gave the alarm. Coppers caught me coming out in the alley.'

Percy examined his finger-nails rather sourly.

'I got six months for that little job. I suppose it was all experience, as my old dad used to say.'

'Was he – was he – er, *one*, too?'

'What, the old man? Coo, no. Real stick in the mud 'e was, fifty years in the same bakery. Died the day after he retired.'

'And have you been *there* – other times?'

'What, jug you mean? That's the trouble, lady. Four times altogether. Last time was eighteen months. That was bad, seemed to go on for ever.'

'But why –'

Percy raised an admonishing finger.

'Now, there you go. Why do I do it? Well, I tell you, lady, I sometimes wonders meself. Often's the time when I think of myself leading a nice quiet strictly above-board life. Why, I 'ad one of these moods only last week. So what do I do? I tries for a job – yes, a real ordinary above-board job. Do you think anyone'll take me on? A bloke what's done four stretches! Not a chance, lady. So, I asks you, 'ow's a fellow to go straight?' Percy looked quite indignant.

'It's not fair, I tell you. I don't know where I'd be if it weren't for my trade, as you might say.'

'I see,' said Miss Meakin, trying very hard to do so but feeling there was something wrong somewhere. It suddenly occurred to her that she was sitting on a public park bench beside a burglar. She peered surreptitiously up and down the pathway almost expecting to see some figure of authority, a policeman or one of the many under-managers of Goodforalls Stores, bearing down upon her with an angry, accusing look.

'Ah, well.' Percy stirred noisily. 'Don't want to burden you with my troubles. It ain't such a bad life really, mind you. It's only that now and then I gets a bit depressed. You know, a feller gets a mood ... That's why I was in to you this morning buying one of them old wills – funny thing, but I've found that a real good cure for depresshun. I just makes out me last will and testament, fill it all out proper-like. And, d'you know, soon as I've done that I feels much brighter, and then I tear it up again ... I'll be getting along then now. Thanks for the sandwiches.'

Miss Meakin flushed guiltily, ashamed of her surreptitious glances. She put out a hesitant, fussy hand to restrain Percy from rising.

'Please don't go.'

'Now then ... you ain't going to call a policeman? He wouldn't believe you anyway,' said Percy defiantly.

'No, I'm sure he wouldn't.' Miss Meakin twisted a handkerchief between her fingers. 'I – er – dear me – er – I –'

'Well?'

'Couldn't you, perhaps, I mean if you made an effort ... I quite realise how difficult it is, but I'm sure you'd be much happier if you – you gave it all up and made a fresh start. An honest one, of course. It worries me to think of you living this *uncertain* sort of life.'

'Oh, I don't know about uncertain,' said Percy. 'It's keeping on the straight and narrow that makes things so uncertain. Now you take the last few days, when I've been laying off the jobs. What 'appens? I'm left stone cold and broke. Not a square meal since yesterday.'

'Goodness,' said Miss Meakin worriedly. She fumbled into her bag. 'Please let me –'

'You can save your charity, miss.' Percy raised an authoritative hand. He looked positively stern. 'I'm not in the 'abit of borrowing.' In a sense Miss Meakin felt Percy meant what he said. She was greatly impressed.

'But how will you eat?'

It was quite simple, explained Percy. There was a certain house in a certain road. He happened to know the owners were away for the day and wouldn't be back until late at night. He was going round there now, casual like, of course. He would go round to the tradesman's entrance and then with the persuasion of a little instrument he had tucked away in his pocket he would insert himself into the house, and then – hey presto, take your choice. Why, Percy shrugged nonchalantly, if the worst came to the worst he was bound to find some food. Mind you, this wasn't his usual way of working. Oh no, he always preferred night-time. But that was what trying to go straight did to you – put you in predicaments such as this, where you had to act fast or else go hungry. Well, there it was. He hoped he hadn't bored Miss Meakin. But it had seemed to him she had a kind face …

'Oh, dear,' said Miss Meakin. 'It all seems such a pity. I wish you didn't have to do it.'

Percy patted her sympathetically on the arm.

'There, there, miss. No fault of yours. Fact is it's cheered me up no end being able to 'ave a good talk with you, like this. Given me back my confidence, you might say. Don't wonder but what I shan't 'ave a lucky 'aul this afternoon. Don't you worry, miss.'

'Oh, but I shall worry all the time,' said Miss Meakin. 'Supposing you get caught? I shan't be able to have any peace of mind until I know if you're all right.'

'Well, tell you what,' said Percy indulgently. 'If it's going to worry you all that much, what say I drop you a line just to let you know I'm OK? Or tell you what – are you on the phone?'

Miss Meakin supposed she was on the phone, boarding-houses usually were, but she had never had occasion to require the number. She fished in her bag and found one of her landlady's business cards, with a phone number.

'Righto,' said Percy cheerfully, carefully pocketing the card. (Through Miss Meakin's mind ran a film-reel, policeman bending over the body of the slain robber, some hawk-nosed detective retrieving a small piece of paper that had fluttered out as the body was lifted, aha, what was this, 10 Everard Grove, guess that was his hide-out, send a van round at once and pick up the occupants ...)

'I'll give you a buzz this evening.' Percy nodded. 'So long for now.'

And almost before Miss Meakin knew it he was walking away, ears flapping in the breeze, hat tilted back on head, looking really like any other nondescript young man.

She looked down at her unread book, her emptied bag of sandwiches.

'Dear me,' she said in a tone of considerable misgiving. Then, seeing from her watch that she was already ten minutes over her lunch hour, she grabbed up her things and scuttled away. It was bad enough having an unrepentant burglar on her hands without the risk of one of those icy reprimands so beloved of Mr Pickering.

That evening Miss Meakin arrived home out of breath from an unusually hurried journey. It was her normal habit to creep up three flights of stairs to her solitary attic-room rather as a mouse returning from some dangerous expedition. She was terrified of her landlady, Mrs Rowlandson, a large blowsy woman who wandered about the house in a faded black and gold kimono and smelt strongly of whisky. The last thing Miss Meakin could have imagined herself doing was knocking a firm rat-tat on the door of Mrs Rowlandson's room.

Mrs Rowlandson opened the door a few inches and peered out curiously.

'What's the matter, dearie? Friday's rent day.'

'Er, I haven't come about the rent, Mrs Rowlandson. I was just wondering if – perhaps – you might have had a message for me? I was expecting a message from a – a friend,' Miss Meakin mumbled. 'A telephone message.'

Mrs Rowlandson's bushy eyebrows tilted to strange angles. Then, as Miss Meakin watched in some fascination, a thick blue-veined eyelid closed in a leering wink. There was a breeze delicately flavoured with whisky as Mrs Rowlandson chuckled.

'Well, well, Miss Meakin. A gentleman friend, perhaps?'

'Oh, no, nothing like that, Mrs Rowlandson. It's just a message from a bur –' Miss Meakin checked herself just in time. She blushed. 'Well, yes, it would probably be from a gentleman.'

Mrs Rowlandson's other eyelid closed and opened.

'So sorry, dearie. No one's rung up yet. But don't you fret. The night is young, eh?'

And with a final nod of womanly understanding, Mrs Rowlandson returned to the alcoholic-conditioned mysteries of her room.

For a while Miss Meakin hovered about in the gloom of the narrow hallway with her eyes glued hopefully on the telephone, which she had discovered standing somewhat publicly on a ledge opposite the dining-room door. She was disconcerted by the appearance in quick succession of Mr Cater, the bank cashier who occupied the room below her, Miss Bailey, the insurance typist who had the room across the landing, and Mr Olsworthy, the chemist, a companion of Mr Cater's on the second floor. As each one passed Miss Meakin was forced to shrink herself against the wall, and the knowledge that she was blushing furiously impelled her to mumble something unintelligible about the telephone. She did not know whether it was her imagination, but her words seemed only to attract increased attention. While Mr Cater did not actually wink there was a suggestive gleam behind his pince-nez. And while neither Mr Olsworthy nor Miss Bailey *said* anything they both looked back at her twice before disappearing upstairs – which somehow seemed more pointed than if they had spoken. The sound of Mrs Rowlandson emerging from her room, humming some strident and obviously vulgar ditty, unnerved Miss Meakin completely and with a last regretful look she hurried upstairs.

In her room she spent a miserable evening trying to occupy herself with making a meal, reading a book, knitting, listening to a very subdued wireless – her ears always sharply tuned for the ringing of the telephone bell. Not unnaturally it sounded some half a dozen times during the evening, and on each occasion Miss Meakin flashed out of the door and down three flights of stairs to be the first to pick up the receiver. After the seventh experience of hearing a strange voice ask for one of the other boarders she began to lose heart. And so when Percy finally rang up at eleven o'clock it was Mrs Rowlandson, sweating and greasy in her kimono, who grunted upstairs, tapped at the door and said:

'Your gentleman friend is inquiring for you, Miss Meakin ... Better late than never, eh, dearie?'

As Miss Meakin scuttled down the stairs she had an uneasy impression that one by one the doors of the other bedrooms were opening behind her, that Mr Cater and Mr Olsworthy and all the others were peeping out with leering winks and nodding to each other: 'That's Miss Meakin's *gentleman* friend on the telephone. She's a bit of a dark horse, eh?'

So when she picked up the receiver she was not only breathless but incoherent, and kept repeating what Percy said as if she could not quite grasp the meaning.

'You say you've done it? ...

'You're quite safe? ...

'It was money for jam? ...

'Not even a watchman?'

Here Miss Meakin eased her wound-up feelings by giving way to a nearly hysterical peal of laughter.

''Ullo, 'ullo?' said Percy. 'What's the joke, lady? It's not funny really, you know. Takes it out of a fellow. Supposing there'd been a dog? There often is.'

'A dog?' repeated Miss Meakin, thus, had she but known it, completely mystifying Mrs Rowlandson as she listened, leaning over the banisters.

'Yes. Dogs don't like burglars. I remember being half killed by an Alsatian on a job in Brixton.' Percy sounded a little impatient.

'Well, I said I'd ring you ...'

'Wait,' said Miss Meakin. 'What are you going to do now?'

'Me? I'm off for a lovely long sleep between clean sheets for a night or two.' Percy became expansive at the thought. His voice conveyed no suspicion of redeeming shame.

Miss Meakin was by now acutely aware of Mrs Rowlandson's kimono-ends billowing out between two balustrades. She was convinced that her fellow boarders were leaning over other banisters. She sank her voice to a tiny whisper.

'Before you go, I was wondering –'

'What's that?'

'I said, I was wondering if we could have another talk. I feel very upset to think of – of you know what. Perhaps – perhaps –' Miss Meakin's whirling brain grasped a wispy prospect. 'Perhaps I can think of some way of helping you to get employment.'

'Perhaps.'

Percy did not sound very keen. But he agreed to be on the embankment at lunch-time the next day. And with that prospect and the knowledge that at least for a night he would be safely tucked between clean sheets, Miss Meakin felt sufficiently relieved to be able to go to bed and sleep peacefully.

For a woman who had never had the initiative to seek any new employment for herself, Miss Meakin made a remarkably tenacious effort to do so on Percy's behalf. The next morning she went out early in order to call at an employment agency whose creaking gilt sign she passed every day. When she met Percy at lunch, sharing with him the extra sandwiches she had prudently brought, she was able to present him with opportunities to be interviewed for employment as a lift-man at a local hotel, as a commissionaire at her own pet Regal, or as a milk-roundsman.

Percy rejected the cinema job at once, but expressed unexpected interest in the other two jobs.

'Might do quite well on the inside of a hotel,' he said, rubbing his chin. 'Though I reckon the milk job would be more reliable. Just think what a fine way it would be of finding out who was at home and who wasn't.' He grinned at Miss Meakin. 'If you know what I mean.'

Miss Meakin understood only too well what he meant, and found it most reprehensible. She decided to scrap all three jobs and to spend more thought on selecting for Percy work in which temptation could not possibly be put in his way. After all, she thought with a curious motherly softening of the heart which came on her whenever she thought of Percy, he could not help being weak, poor boy. It was probably the result of a bad upbringing. Upon her had fallen the duty of guiding him back to a more honest way of life.

With some difficulty Miss Meakin produced openings for employment as a hospital porter, a workhouse gardener, a worker at the sewage depot and a trolley-bus driver.

'That would involve quite a long training,' she remarked doubtfully of the last job. 'That is, unless you've ever driven a trolley-bus?'

'No, I ain't. And I've no intention of doing so, lady. Nor none of the others you mention. They don't sound civilised to me.' Percy drew himself up. The previous night he had a done a successful crib on a doctor's house and absconded with £30 in cash as well as some trinkets and rings. He was feeling rather proud of himself. 'After all, lady, you must remember I've certain standards.'

Miss Meakin sighed, but had no heart to argue. Much of her mental strength had been used up on the previous evening conducting a whispered conversation with Percy while Mrs Rowlandson leaned with effusive friendliness against the wall by the phone alternatively winking and cocking an inquisitive ear. Afterwards she had made pressing invitations to come and join her in a little drop, and Miss Meakin had found it necessary to screw up all her moral and even physical courage to extricate herself. Truly, her life at the boarding-house had taken on a noticeable change. People who had never acknowledged her existence now seemed to go out of their way to do so. At meal times she was convinced that when her eyes were bent demurely upon the table many other eyes studied her covertly. It would have been rather enjoyable, she could not help thinking, this becoming, what was the phrase? – a cynosure of all eyes – were it not for the reason. It was indeed a matter of uplift to have a gentleman friend, but it was quite another matter to accommodate a burglar friend. Nevertheless, such was the persuasive intrusion of Mrs Rowlandson alone, Miss Meakin felt she must provide an explanation of her telephone caller. He was an *elderly* gentleman she emphasised rather primly, thus clarifying, as she imagined, the purity of the relationship. He was a man of very lofty ideals. They went for long walks along the river. They visited museums, and the cinema if there was a serious film. On Sundays he went to chapel at least twice, said Miss Meakin with great satisfaction.

When Mrs Rowlandson announced *her* intention of accompanying them on the following Sunday – 'It would do an old sinner like me the world of good, dearie, and perhaps your friend will have some words of advice for me!' – Miss Meakin had to explain hastily that her friend went to a church in his own district. And where was that, dearie? In Barnet, said Miss Meakin wildly, dimly recollecting it as a suburb on the distant other side of London. Why, dearie, my sister lives in Barnet. Now, I wonder if she would know your friend? What's his name, I'll ask her ...

And so it went on. Miss Meakin produced a name out of her now fertile imagination. Mr Arbuthnot. She could not think where she got the name from, but after a while concluded it had come more or less from Heaven. At any rate she grew extremely fond of it. She felt it conveyed the impression of some strange ideal personage – a combination, it once occurred to her, of a less malefactory Percy and a somewhat sweetened memory of her father. Mr Arbuthnot was, obviously, a Scotsman – when Mrs Rowlandson, after answering the telephone, remarked accusingly that he didn't sound like a Scotsman, Miss Meakin explained deftly that he had settled in London in his early youth.

'But he has a kilt, you know for – special occasions,' she added with that unexpected flash of daring which had come to her of late.

Possibly such remarks were part of a new-found exhibitionism arising out of Miss Meakin's changed status. For there was no doubt but she found it refreshing to have both Mr Cater and Mr Olsworthy bidding her hearty good mornings when she came down to breakfast. And there had been several occasions recently when Mr Cater had walked with her as far as his bus stop which unfortunately, he said with a slight bow, lay before her station.

Miss Meakin would have felt encouraged by all this activity were it not for the grim reality of the telephone calls. She could not help feeling that Percy was unnecessarily active in his profession. On an average he rang up three times in a week, and it had become understood that he met her for lunch every Friday. On these occasions Percy was always a model of politeness and innocence, occasionally earnest in his consideration of the various proposals of employment which Miss Meakin still managed to discover. But on the telephone he invariably sounded jovial, even facetious, elaborating for Miss Meakin's benefit the most detailed account of the particular burglary which he had just carried out. Sometimes he referred with pride to the newspapers of a day or two back, where she could find an interesting account of his last little job. 'It says,' Percy would read out, ' "the police are confident they will shortly make an arrest".' Then he would guffaw loudly, so loudly that the echoes would sound across the hallway and into the dining-room and Miss Meakin was forced in self-defence to burst into hearty laughter herself, as if she and the telephone were sharing some great, but, of course, perfectly proper joke.

'I like to hear you laughing, Miss Meakin,' said Mr Cater the next morning. 'It gives one a new faith in life.'

But when she saw Percy the next day, Miss Meakin's face was most unamused. It was really most disappointing, she said, that he should still be without employment, and after all the opportunities there had been.

Percy was most anxious to be reasonable.

'You don't understand, lady. One breath of my having been in prison – whizz-bang, no job.' Percy looked woeful. Then, with a quick sideways look, he said nonchalantly:

'Tell you what, lady, what price getting me in with your firm?'

'Goodness,' said Miss Meakin. 'Why – I've never thought of that.'

'Well … it's an idea, ain't it?' Percy lowered his voice. 'Struck me we might skip any reference to my past career, ha-ha!'

'Yes, indeed,' said Miss Meakin without stopping to wonder why Percy had not thought of such an idea before.

The more she thought about it the more Miss Meakin became buoyed up with a surge of new excitement. A job for Percy at Goodforalls Stores would mean more than a job anywhere else. She would be near at hand, able to encourage him through the dark hours, to egg him towards the golden horizon of an honest man's life.

'I shall certainly speak to Mr Pickering this very afternoon,' she said briskly.

Mr Pickering was obviously intrigued.

'A friend of *yours*, Miss Meakin?' he repeated, as if becoming aware of her existence for the first time. 'Mmmmh. Well, well. We must see what we can do, mustn't we? Mind you, I can't promise anything. But' – expansively – 'I will use what influence I may possess.'

And Percy, surprisingly, made a good impression. This was almost a new Percy to Miss Meakin; his suit neatly creased and brushed, his hands well-washed, his face clean-shaven, about him just the right air of respectful deference. Miss Meakin felt sure that he would do very well as a third assistant, or even a second assistant – say in the men's clothing or perhaps the toy department?

But Percy evidently wished to start at the bottom.

'You see, it's like this, sir. I been used to a lot of night work. You might say – sir – I've sort of specialised in that line. Night-watchman, that's been my trade. So I was thinking, maybe I could serve you in that – hem – capacity. You'll find me quite satisfactory, sir.'

'Oh, I'm sure you would, Mr Pickering. He's had some excellent testimonials.'

At first Mr Pickering thought he might like to see these, but the combined enthusiasm of Percy and Miss Meakin carried him into a jovial commitment to employ Percy as a night-watchman to Messrs Goodforalls Stores, hours 9 p.m. to 9 a.m., beginning on the following Monday.

'And you really will be there?' said Miss Meakin as they walked away.

'Why, 'course I will, lady. And many thanks for the help along.'

What Miss Meakin would really like to have asked was, would it mean an end to Percy's more indiscreet activities. She could not help thinking that the occupation of night-watchman was hardly likely to allow Percy much time for nocturnal wanderings. When at the end of the first week there had not been a single phone call from Percy she felt a definite sense of achievement. She used to think affectionately of his lanky figure pacing doggedly around the silent halls and corridors of Goodforalls, like a faithful sentinel. On the Monday she left him a little parcel of food, containing an encouraging note. Her cup of righteous happiness reached its highest level when, during a slack period on the Tuesday, Mr Pickering deigned to murmur, with an approving nod, that her friend was proving himself a willing worker with a real interest in his job. This spurred Miss Meakin into knitting a pair of thick woollen socks for Percy – after all she was sure he must wear them out quickly on his long night walks – and these she left for him with another encouraging note.

But by the middle of the second week she discerned a strange restlessness and dissatisfaction about herself, just when she ought to be feeling eminently pleased with life. She found herself hurrying home anxious to know if there had been a telephone call. When she learnt with expressive disappointment that there had not, she was aware of a certain condescension in Mrs Rowlandson's voice. And was it her imagination that now when Miss Bailey or her friend Miss Atkinson inquired after 'the gentleman friend' and she confessed that she had not heard from him recently – was there just the faintest purring note in their voices? And could it be her fancy that Mr Olsworthy and even Mr Cater, were just a little engrossed in their newspapers when she came in to breakfast?

Miss Meakin felt so depressed at such thoughts that she was almost tempted to leave a note instructing Percy to ring her. Some obstinate pride prevented her doing this, but she certainly concentrated all her mental powers onto wishing that Percy would do so. Alas, Percy remained silent that night, and the next night, and again the Saturday night.

But on the Sunday night he did ring. An appropriate night, Miss Meakin thought as she joyfully ran down the stairs at Mrs Rowlandson's call, for everybody was always at home on that night and the telephone call could not fail to be noted.

She greeted Percy quite affectionately. She spoke of her anxiety about his health, about her hopes that he had a good trip north. She was even steeling herself to say something gay about meeting to-morrow when Percy broke in.

'Look, lady, save it up. I'm in an 'urry, 'ell of an 'urry. It's probably cutting my own throat to waste time like this. But I promised you I'd allus ring you up and give you the tip, like.

'Well,' Percy's voice sank a little, and Miss Meakin, aware of a certain cold foreboding, pressed the receiver closer to her ear. 'Well, I thought I'd just let you know. I just done a job, see?'

'Oh, Percy!' exclaimed Miss Meakin, exasperation over-coming her normal reticence. 'After all my efforts. After I thought it was all ended ...'

Behind various doors Mrs Rowlandson, Mr Cater and Mr Olsworthy pricked up their ears.

'Now, lady, don't blow off. You know 'ow it is. Once a crook, allus a crook, I suppose.' Percy sounded peculiarly unsorry for himself. 'There it is, lady. But anyway, 'ere's something to make you feel 'appier. This is the *biggest* job little Percy's ever done. If I told you 'ow much you'd probably faint.'

'I don't want to hear another word. I'm most, most disappointed,' Miss Meakin said sharply. 'It's altogether a *great* blow to me. I feel I can't help you any more.'

Upstairs Mrs Rowlandson, Mr Cater and Mr Olsworthy raised their eyebrows and nodded understandingly.

'Okey-doke, lady, I can take an 'int. I won't bother you no more then. Just thought I'd put your mind at rest.' Percy paused and then said, as if with some embarrassment. 'You'll be hearing all about it, I've no doubt. Don't you worry now, will you? And – and –' He whispered the last sentence. 'Remember, you don't know anything about *me*. I've gorn away, see?'

'And a good job, too!'

'Ah, well, there it is. Human nature. So long, lady, and many thanks.'

Miss Meakin nearly said good-bye and good-riddance, but managed to restrain herself and make a dignified return to her room. Once safely behind the door she quickly found her anger disappearing and being replaced by a great wave of self-pity. No more telephone calls. No more being the cynosure of all eyes. An end to the pleasant new dream world ... Unable to control the sad reflections any longer she threw herself on to the bed sobbing bitterly. So bitterly that she did not hear Mr Cater's gentle tap on the door and was only aware of his tall presence when he was standing nervously beside her, stammering out an apology for intruding mixed up with an earnest request that he should be allowed to be of any help he could. Could he perhaps make Miss Meakin some tea?

Miss Meakin, fussily drying her eyes, admitted that she would indeed welcome some tea. And she was most impressed at the competence with which Mr Cater disappeared and reappeared bearing a hot, steaming teapot and some cups.

It was when she was drinking her second cup and feeling greatly refreshed that Mr Cater ventured to remark how it was always a source of great sadness to him some people could behave so unkindly to their friends. Yes, indeed, Miss Meakin thoroughly agreed with him. Soon Mr Cater was hazarding that some men were brutes and again Miss Meakin quite agreed.

And by the time Mr Cater had tactfully suggested that Miss Meakin might care to accompany him to the pictures on the following night, Miss Meakin had quite forgotten about the waywardness of a rather mythical young man with flapping ears.

So that the next morning when she read in her newspaper that a daring robbery of goods and cash to the value of £5,000 had been carried out at the premises of Messrs Goodforalls Stores, Ltd., she remained entirely unperturbed, even at the thought of the icy things Mr Pickering was likely to have to say. After all she had tried her utmost to make Percy an honest man. Meanwhile, thought Miss Meakin, with a rosy and excited peep into the immediate future, Mr Cater was undoubtedly cheap at the price.

IV

Sea Changes

Max reckoned to make the trip in the early spring when the weather at sea might be a little more reliable. There was no desperate hurry; the long search was over at last, he had found the boat he had dreamed about all those years, paid over the money, and signed the papers. Now she lay waiting for him further up the South coast; he could afford to take his time over the ultimate consummation of bringing her round to Falmouth.

'The first weekend in May will do fine.'

His wife was less calm and collected about the matter. Indeed, she behaved excitably, effusively, almost as if it was her boat, he thought irritably. She was a small, rather vital woman with a mop of reddish hair and an open, rather piquant doll's face; she had large bright brown eyes, which in a state of emotion seemed to shine brighter than ever.

'Oh, I can't wait to get aboard. Can't we go sooner than that?'

As he shook his head she pouted.

'Oh, don't be a meanie.'

In a way that was at once painfully obvious and yet delectably familiar she came up to him and inserted herself into his arms, pressing against his body provocatively.

'You really are the limit.' He managed to sound cross. 'Why, you were against the whole idea.'

She looked at him mockingly.

'Maybe I didn't believe it would ever happen.'

He hesitated. Perhaps she could hardly be blamed. It was something he had talked about endlessly, boring no doubt, ever since they had been married and settled down to run a small successful guest house on the South Cornish coast. In the evenings he used to lean over the harbour wall and dream romantically of seeing his own boat lying there at anchor. No doubt it had all become something of a myth in Di's more practical eyes. Indeed it was only because of an unexpected inheritance that he had been able to make myth reality.

'Well, it has happened,' he said with some satisfaction. And then, more firmly, 'And we're going to bring her down very soon.'

It was a little more complicated than that. The boat was a large one, a sixty-foot converted fishing vessel – large enough, in fact, to go round the world if need be. It wasn't the sort of boat he could have handled on his own even if he wanted to, and he felt the need for moral support extending beyond Di.

In the end there were six of them making the trip: himself and his wife, a professional skipper they decided to hire for the occasion, another married couple, Alan and May Gibbs, and a tall, dark, rather solitary girl called Merle who had somehow drifted into their life recently.

The skipper's name was Pratt, Ted Pratt, and they picked him up on the way to Southampton, on a corner of the Exeter bypass. At first sight he was rather as they had expected, a sturdy, weather-beaten-looking man in his early forties, with the bright blue eyes of a seagoing man; he even wore the rather conventional yachting cap, tilted at a slight rakish angle. When he talked, too, it was the sort of knowledgeable, professional seamen's talk they might have expected; but then gradually, as the long hours slipped by and everyone relaxed a little, they realized with relief that Ted Pratt had a neat sense of humour and wasn't really half as well defined as he seemed at first glance. Although he had delivered boats all over Europe and had only recently come back for his thirtieth trip to the Mediterranean, he remained curiously unaffected by what must be the familiarity of his job. Somehow, they sensed, he remained still a romantic about the life at sea – and indeed, as his engaging, rather warm personality unfolded, they began to find something romantic in the man himself. There was an impressive, half-hidden strength about his movements, a piercing look in his eyes, that combined gradually to make his a compelling presence.

They reached the boatyard about four o'clock. There was a waspish fresh wind blowing down the river about which Max had to restrain a secret, uneasy feeling. He had been studying a lot of books about seamanship and navigation and he knew that a strong wind was not a good omen. His spirits weren't raised by the old man in oilskins and sou'wester who rowed them out to where the boat was moored in deep water.

'Worse now than it's been all winter. Look at those white horses out there!'

But then the long-term worries disappeared before the immediacy of at last seeing the boat – his boat, his very *own* boat – lying snugly at her moorings, somehow more graceful, even more beautiful, than he had ever imagined. He was surprised at his own emotional reactions; the feeling of tender possessiveness was almost akin to some secret passion a man might feel for a woman.

He tried to control the tremor in his voice.

'Well, what do you think of her?'

'Very nice.' Ted stood, feet astride, in the skiff, eyeing the boat with professional interest. 'A good sea boat, I can see that. Let's get aboard and have a good look round.'

The others, Max could see, were suitably impressed. Indeed he was impressed again himself; he had forgotten quite how large and solid the boat was. Now as, proudly, he guided them round the wheel-house, down in the saloon, finally into the enormous engine room dominated by the sleek brass-topped diesel engine, he glowed with a new sense of proprietorship.

'Of course, she needs a few things done, a good clean-up, repaint, and so on, but first we thought we'd take her down nearer home.'

He joined Alan and May, leaning over the rails and watching the stream running fast across the bows. They were a younger couple than Di and he, and tended to look up to them in some way; he supposed this was what why, unconsciously, Di and he gravitated towards them. Alan was a librarian in a nearby town, May a schoolteacher. They were one of those couples who seemed to have become rather alike, both tall and slim and good-looking in a sensitive sort of way, with fine delicate features, high cheekbones, fair hair, rather sad eyes; sometimes, he found with amusement, they seemed like brother and sister. Often he had difficulty in remembering they were man and wife, with a carnal relationship.

Now they were unexpectedly gay and elated.

'Maxy, you didn't give us any idea –'

'She's enormous!'

He smiled.

'You like her?'

'Like her?' May half turned her head and the breeze caught her blonde hair, spilling it out in a sudden look of abandon he had never noticed before. She laughed up at him, and somehow he almost felt her youth entering into him, a free gift on a special day.

'I adore her.'

Smiling, he put a fatherly arm around Alan's slim shoulders.

'I thought you might. That's why we asked you along. Mind you –' he wagged a warning finger '– there'll be plenty of work to do.'

He was content, though, to leave the organizing of the work side to Ted Pratt, who was already way down in the engine room checking over the engine and priming the gasoline starters. Di was down there too: he caught a glimpse of her crouched in a corner, watching with that curiously intense manner of hers, so that you felt for the moment her whole being was engrossed. It was one of her most engaging yet disturbing characteristics, this ability to lose herself in the moment.

He walked thoughtfully down the long sloping deck to the aft of the boat and found Merle sitting nonchalantly on the deck rail, kicking her heels, looking, in her bright blue jeans and huge woolly red jersey, like the boy she almost was. She was something of a mystery, really. She had appeared in their little seaside town the previous summer along with the usual crowd of teenage students and beatniks on holiday, but when the tide had washed them away again back to their studies and winter jobs, Merle had remained. For a time she had worked as a waitress in one of the cafes, but when that closed down and she was out of work he and Di had taken pity on her and offered her a room at the top of their house, in return for some help about the house. It was a tiny, tucked-away attic room that somehow suited Merle's strange, withdrawn, personality.

She spent long hours up there, sitting by the window that looked out over the harbour, sometimes drawing charcoal pictures of the romantic view. Both Max and Di had been impressed with the drawings, but Merle herself didn't seem any more interested in them than she was in any other material things. She was a dreamer, a romantic, a lost soul. Max supposed that he and Di felt towards her some secret kind of parental fondness, as a substitution for the child they had wanted but so far never had. Something like that, anyway.

'Penny for them,' he said.

Merle's dark eyes glistened.

'They're worth more than that.'

'Sixpence then? A shilling!'

She pouted and laughed.

'I'm glad you brought me. Thanks.'

He sat beside her, turning to look along the line of the ship, from that position seeming even bigger than ever.

'It should be an interesting trip,' he said.

Merle clasped her hands over her knee, rocking backwards and forwards as if careless of the fact she might easily tip back into the water.

'Aren't you excited?'

'Of course.'

She peered at him, pushing away a mass of dark hair.

'I don't just mean about the trip. I mean about everything.'

She paused as if to lend effect to her next remark.

'I mean, it's all your very own – a boat of your own. Why, it's fantastic. It will change your whole life.'

'Do you think so?' He looked at her in genuine surprise. 'What makes you think that?'

She did not answer immediately, and he found himself instead finding the reply for himself. Of course she was right, really. It was too gigantic, too enormous a new part of his life to be lightly put aside. Even financially it threatened to be crippling; he had been warned again and again about the high cost of maintenance of a boat like this. But there it was, he had taken the decisive step of commitment – he and Di, for in the end she had seemed suddenly to join in with him, after holding back critically. What might it all involve, now?

'Look at the waves!' Merle had turned and was kneeling,

hanging her head over the side. 'There's no end to them, here
one moment, gone the next.' She pointed downstream, to
where the tide rapidly rushed past boats moored further up,
and along toward the faint line of the open sea.

'Funny, soon we shall be out there too, out with the sea
dragons and the sharks and the – the –' She paused and
laughed, suddenly standing up and stretching her arms wide as
if in obeisance to some unknown God. 'Out with all the
mermaids!'

He laughed with her.

'Perhaps that's why you've come, really. Perhaps you're one
of them.'

He went back to the wheelhouse, taking the curious image with
him of a Merle mermaid, then losing it in the task of making
sure everything was shipshape. Ted was up from the engine
room now, having started the big diesel, which hummed away
purposefully below.

'We might as well be making a start. It's too late to go far
tonight, but we can make Yarmouth.'

With Ted at the wheel, Max like a shadow at his side, the big
boat headed down the river, its enormous weight gliding
effortlessly through the disturbed water. Soon they were out of
the river into the wide estuary of the Solent. Heading into
more open water Max felt a tremendous surge of elation
spreading over him. He looked round for Di, caught sight of
her, changed to a bright green open-necked blouse and jeans,
sitting near the bow. He opened the side window and called
out.

'We're off.'

Di turned, grinning. She had what he called her young look
shining out of her: suddenly she looked exuberant and
exhilarated. He could almost imagine her as he had first seen
her all those years ago.

He turned casually just in time to catch the absorbed gaze of
Ted Pratt fixed in the same direction. The brown face was
slightly wrinkled, as if the eyes were staring with particular
intensity, to make quite sure of the object seen. As if, Max
thought detachedly, he was identifying some strange ship at
sea.

Seemingly unembarrassed by Max's attention, Ted Pratt grinned.

'Your wife looks pretty well at home.'

'Yes.' Max hesitated, unable to put his finger on a strange sense of unease; he decided it must be his imagination and went on.

'Of course she's never been to sea before.'

'Oh, I can see that.' Ted Pratt cocked his head on one side, pushing back his faded yachting cap, as if considering some problem of grave importance. 'But she'll be all right – you can see that.' He looked at Max very quickly, then away again. 'Quite a sport, your missus, I'd say.'

'Oh, yes.' Max laughed dubiously. 'Yes, quite.'

They stood side by side for half an hour or so until the boat was well down the channel, then Ted spoke suddenly.

'Like a turn at the wheel?'

Max hesitated, then took two of the big curved wooden spokes in his hands.

'All right. Shall I keep her on this course?'

'Yes, south by south-west. See that headland over there? Keep her almost dead on that, she'll be all right.'

Ted Pratt nodded and then went out onto the deck. For a moment or two Max watched his broad figure curiously as he padded around, checking the ropes, then he found himself losing interest before the more compelling and immediate task of holding the boat on her course.

It was not the first time he had steered a boat, but the first time he had steered his own boat. Once again he was surprised at the enormity of his feeling of possessiveness. He gripped the wheel more tightly, correcting it at each attempt of the boat to head slightly one way or another. Then, when he felt more in control, he wedged himself at one side of the wheel, leaning against the open window, staring out like every other captain down the ages, at the long white-tipped waves sweeping down towards him.

'My boat,' he thought, sweetly. 'My boat …'

A little later, to take over for the entry to Yarmouth, Ted came back into the wheelhouse. He whistled a tune as he spun the wheel around, heading for the harbour entry.

'Had quite a talk with your missus.' His face split into an appreciative grin. 'Fond of a chat, isn't she?'

Max nodded.

'She's all right? Not feeling sick or anything?'

Ted gave a guffaw.

'No, not her. She's a tough one, she is.'

He peered ahead and nodded at Merle, who had come up to the front.

'How about her? It is a she, isn't it?'

There was no malice in Ted's voice, and Max answered the question with a mild smile.

'Yes, she's a she. That's Merle. We're very fond of her. She's a bit of a lost soul really.'

'Aye,' said Ted Pratt, but casually as if it would be of no further interest. 'She's that all right.'

Max felt almost obliged to say something further in defence of Merle, but really could not think what. At last he went out of the wheelhouse and over to where the girl stood, her hair blown out in the evening breeze.

'You know what?' he said coming up behind her. 'You'd make a very nice figurehead for the boat.'

Merle laughed, half turned her head, then shrugged and stared ahead again.

Now they were very near to the harbour entrance. It was almost dark and lights had sprung up in all directions, like people. The others had come on deck now, all except Ted, who stood dutifully at the wheel.

Max turned to observe Alan and May, standing on the starboard side. Like Di, they too had changed, Alan looked slightly incongruous in a fisherman's jersey and old shorts, which revealed his rather spindly legs, and May looked no less unfamiliar in dungarees and a sailcloth top. As he watched, Alan put an arm round May with an awkward movement, and once again it seemed somehow slightly unreal to Max. He looked sharply to see May's reaction, and was surprised to notice that behind her back her fingers had clutched Alan's hand and were squeezing, forcefully, almost as if wishing to hurt. It was the first time he had comprehended that there might really be some subterranean sexual contact between the two of them, and he found the thought curiously provocative.

He went on watching May, looking in some way so innocent
and pure with her blonde hair all awry and her mouth open
and her teeth gleaming – and hardly noticed the professional
and competent way in which Ted brought the big boat through
the lines of small yachts and finally up to a berth at the far
quay.

Instead it was Di who clapped her hands and said:

'Bravo, Ted. You did that jolly well. I think you deserve a
drink – come on, we'll all go and have one.'

They had their first meal aboard the boat late that night,
some lamb chops they had picked up at Southampton on the
way, together with boiled potatoes and peas and fresh fruit
afterwards. To celebrate the occasion they opened two of the
half-dozen bottles of white wine they had asked to have
delivered with the groceries. Max drew the cork and moved
around the tiny but cosy saloon, filling the tall glasses. When
all were ready they raised their glasses and clinked them
vigorously, and drank the cool hock with pleasure.

'Well,' said Max with a smile. 'This makes me feel like some
old-time captain,' – he nodded in deference towards Ted –
'only of course Ted's the real man in charge.'

Ted shrugged his massive shoulders.

'Oh, you'll pick it up soon enough. Main thing to remember
is not to panic. Take your time, never rush in where angels fear
to tread.' He grinned, the smile opening up his tanned face
and making him look curiously young and very attractive.

'Look at me, I've survived, and I've been at sea for twenty
years.'

'Go on,' said Di in her direct way. 'I don't believe it – you're
not that old.'

Ted laughed.

'Oh, but I am – I'm the original old man of the sea.'

Merle leaned forward, tongue between lips.

'Tell me about it – your life at sea. Have you ever been
shipwrecked?'

'Well, now,' said Ted lightly, 'I wouldn't be here if I had,
would I? But I don't mind telling you I've had a few near
escapes. There was a time when I was taking a twenty-four-foot
yacht out to the Med. It was early spring, and everything was
all right until I got round Finistere. And then – I think it was

just by La Rochelle – the most almighty gale sprang up. I had all the topsail out, and just ran before it.'

The rest listened entranced to what, Max could not help suspecting, was fairly matter-of-fact accounts of everyday jobs of yacht delivery. Yet, he had to admit, there was something about Ted's youthful excitement that made even the ordinary seem colourful. As he spoke. Often gesturing with his big brown hands, it was possible somehow to go back in time with him, riding with the winds, bringing some unknown boat safely at last into some strange foreign port. And this knowledge alone seemed to give Ted an aura of the alien, the exotic.

'You really put us to shame,' said May, lighting up a cigarette. 'Alan and I just read about things like this. You do them.'

As she spoke she flashed a secretive look at her husband and Max reflected again what he had never noticed until this trip, how engrossed they were with one another. Strange, he thought, they have been married five years or more, time for the first bloom to wear off, and yet there lay between them, almost visible, some subterranean tension so that all the time, one felt, they were almost painfully aware of one another.

It was different, he thought, with Di and himself. They had achieved a familiarity not of contempt, but perhaps of conceit. After ten years of married life they believed they knew each other inside out, and were probably right – though sometimes, of course, he felt he understood Di better than she understood him – as for instance now. He could sit back sipping his coffee, with one watchful eye observing her every movement, ticking them off almost as predictable. She was drawn, as a moth to a light, always by the new and exciting. He could see she was fascinated, not so much by Ted Pratt as by the strange rather unknown world he represented. Just as, in another more intangible romantic way, Merle would be fascinated. But Merle would always perhaps seek the ethereal, shadowlike unreality; Di was more down to earth and realistic.

'Ah, well.' Ted rose suddenly and stretched himself with a yawn. 'I think I'll just check round the moorings.'

He climbed lithely up the steep companion way.

'Hey, wait a minute!' Di moved after him. 'I could do with a breath of fresh air, too.'

After some hesitation Max went up into the wheelhouse, took down the chart marked Needles to Start Point and began tracing their course for the next day. It was a simple enough passage across to the point, and after taking one or two bearings he put the chart aside. Then, yawning to himself, he went to the wheelhouse door and stared out over the little harbour and the bobbing navigation lights of the other boats. High up in the sky what looked like more navigation lights were really the winking stars of a thousand other planets. He had seen them many times before, but never in quite such circumstances.

Ahead of him, at the bow of the boat, he heard a tinkling laugh from Di, followed by the gruff voice of Ted, telling some story, or recounting some past experience. Diffident, Max did not like to interrupt them. He knew that May and Alan had gone to bed, and as for Merle, she seemed to have vanished into the darkness somewhere. He wondered about her curiously, if she would always be like that, intangible, lost in shadows; he found himself trying in his mind to recreate her face, her strange being, to make her alive – almost out of a perverse pleasure. Then, giving up the attempt, he yawned again and went down to his cabin. He undressed quickly and slipped into the sleeping bag and lay there, the light out, watching the bobbing of lights on the water reflected through the portholes.

A little while later Di came in quietly, and he glimpsed her whiteness as she quickly slipped off her clothes.

'Tired?' he said idly.

'Pretty much.'

'It's all that fresh air.'

He put out a languid hand and touched her gently on one white shoulder as she bent to get into her sleeping bag. For a moment he felt her quiver, and then she turned and bent over him, kissing him briefly on the forehead.

'Goodnight.'

He sighed.

'Goodnight.'

They lay there in their separate sleeping bags, comfortable and tired, for their first night aboard the boat of his dreams.

But somehow sleep was a long time coming.

At six o'clock in the morning Ted was banging on their cabin door, awakening them to the harsh reality of an early start in order to catch the western tide. An hour later they were heading out past the Needles, into a great steady swell of sea. The forecast was not a good one, force five to six, westerlies.

Soon the boat was pitching in a way much more violent than anything they had experienced the previous evening. When they had to alter course to head for Lyme Bay, thus taking the waves on their beam, the rolling began, too, a hideously uncomfortable sensation.

At first they spread themselves about the boat, May and Alan standing up near the bow and watching the white-capped spray, Merle sitting at the stern, Di and Max with Ted in the wheelhouse. Now, a little alarmed by the violence of the sea's motion, the others came in out of the whirling spray. Alan and May had both gone rather quiet, and after a while retired abruptly to their cabin. Merle, too, seemed somehow to withdraw into herself, finally curling up in a corner of the wheelhouse and going to sleep.

Max braced himself in a corner, beside Ted watching the steady way in which the seaman kept the ship on course despite all the buffetings. Behind him he was aware of Di leaning back, looking a little pale. When finally she was sick into a bucket he sought uncomfortably to move over and comfort her – and was promptly sick himself.

'You've survived,' he said wryly to Ted a little while later, when he had recovered somewhat.

'Oh, well, I'm used to it.' Ted absentmindedly turned the boat's head to meet a quite gigantic wave; for a moment the prow rose high in the air, then came crashing down into the trough. 'Mind you, it's quite bad today. If you want to go back, or put in somewhere like Poole, let me know. I don't mind, I'm used to punching on, but it's no use making yourself miserable.'

Max said they would press on, so they headed out past Anvil Point. But the weather, instead of lightening or improving, seemed to worsen, and at last Ted decided they would give up the idea of reaching Brixham and put in at Weymouth. By the time they reached that pleasant sheltered harbour they were all really very glad of the respite.

Once they had moored up at one of the town quays, within sight of the shops of the old part, the sun came out, and they relaxed. Unfortunately, Max felt still rather queasy, and when finally it was decided to forage into the town after an evening meal he felt he could not face the journey.

'It's all right, don't let me spoil the fun. I'll go to bed. I'll be all right in the morning.'

He heard them departing a little while later, their voices raised cheerfully in the relief of being on dry land again. Against his better judgment he raised himself on one elbow and peered out the porthole. Alan and May were already ashore, and walking away down the quayside. He saw Merle following them, looking rather like a stray waif in a long yellow oilskin macintosh, her black hair tousled. Behind her he caught a glimpse of Di stepping gingerly off the boat onto the quay. She turned then, waiting, and a moment later Ted jumped ashore. He, too, paused, looking around to make sure everything was ship-shape, then he tipped his yachting cap back on his head, turned towards Di with a smile and took her by the arm. They walked off in the wake of the others, laughing at something ... and Max watched them thoughtfully until they had disappeared and the quay was silent and alone.

When it was time to leave Weymouth the next morning Ted suggested Max take charge.

'It's the best thing in the world for you – practice. And this is a good berth to leave. You can just unfasten the bow warp and the tide will bring the head round, then cast off aft and away she goes.'

Surprisingly, that's how it went. Max stood, feeling rather important in the wheelhouse, the big spokes resting firmly in his rather nervous grasp, while on deck Ted and Alan with some help from the two women freed the ropes. The big diesel engine was already purring away under his feet, and as the head of the boat swung round with the current he opened the throttle a fraction and felt the faint shudder of added power running through the boat. Once again he was surprised at the intensity of the feeling of proprietary pleasure that ran through him. He supposed it was a little after the style of the reactions of men who broke in young colts – only not really, for this was an old and wise colt. Yet he was, in some subtle way, gradually taking control. Yes, that was it.

Feeling more confident than ever, indeed for him positively elated, Max took his boat down the narrow channel to the opening of Weymouth harbour and then out around the red buoy that led toward Portland Bill.

'We'll have to watch the race there,' said Ted warningly. 'But I think we'll risk going inside, it saves a lot of time.'

Max nodded, holding firmly to the wheel.

'Are you all right?' said Ted. 'Want me to take over?'

'No, I'm fine.' He gave a sudden almost shy smile, as of one wanting to share an intimacy. 'Matter of fact, I wouldn't mind steering all the way.'

'Suits me,' said Ted. He began whistling to himself, moving about the wheelhouse a little, restless at his sudden leisure.

'I'll be OK,' said Max. 'You go out and get some fresh air.'

The rest of the long sunny afternoon he guided the boat across the wide stretch of Lyme Bay, with the land ever disappearing further and further on the horizon until at one stage they were nearly twenty miles out to sea. It was quite rough, though not as bad as the previous day, and now they had their sea legs anyway and were more able to enjoy the trip. Max had the window down so that he could see clearly ahead of him, and found himself enjoying scanning the wide horizon, sometimes spying a passing ocean liner, sometimes, nearer at hand, the white sails of a yacht. He noticed with interest the sensation of being completely cut off from the outside world, the sense indeed of being master not only of his ship but, truly, of his fate. He felt a glow of well-being, and, full of that spirit, leaned out of the window and called out to Merle, who was leaning pensively over the rail.

She turned, pushing back her long black hair and smiling up at him.

'Thinking about mermaids again?' he teased.

She laughed.

'Not exactly.'

'Come up to the wheelhouse and talk a little.' He smiled. 'It gets lonely for the captain.'

She nodded and came around to the door at the side. As she opened it the boat breasted a big swell and then rolled slightly on coming down, and Merle nearly fell back. Quickly Max darted across and held out a helping hand. In her momentary fear she clung to him like a vice and he felt her nails drawing blood, but he held on grimly.

Afterwards, in the wheelhouse, she was very contrite.

'Your poor hand – I'm terribly sorry.'

He shook his head.

'It's nothing.'

She insisted on taking out a small handkerchief and cleaning the tiny cuts. As she did so she held his hand lightly in her own and he noticed the coolness of her hand. It was a white, almost fastidious hand, and against it his own looked huge and dirty. He began to apologize, but she cut him short.

'It's my fault. You were only helping, and I hurt you.'

As she spoke he was aware of a sense of timelessness, as if in some way everything was standing still and there was just the boat pitching up and down and the two of them in the wheelhouse: and all the time – the first time since he had seen Merle that there had been any kind of physical contact between them – the consciousness of his hand resting in hers, the touch there, secret, meaningful, continuing.

At last he seemed to emerge from a kind of coma; he blinked and smiled.

'That's often the way, isn't it?' he said, trying to sound flippant. 'How does the song go, eh?'

But he broke off then, remembering indeed the words of the song: 'You always hurt the one you love ...' He looked sideways at the dark, unknown girl beside him. Strange that she had always seemed so remote, so distant, and yet that now, all at once, he was so much aware of her physical presence. He studied with pleasure the profile of her face, admiring the strong, sensual lips and bold cheekbones.

'Are you still enjoying the trip?'

She leaned beside him, staring out the window, seeing – though of this he could not be sure – exactly what he saw. She spoke almost in a whisper.

'Oh, yes – more, more, much more than I expected.'

His next remark sounded rather foolish as soon as he had uttered it.

'You're not lonely?'

She looked at him with wide-open eyes.

'Lonely? Good heavens, no. Why should I be?' She gestured all around, whether at the ocean or the boat, he could not be sure. 'I'm not alone anyway, am I?'

He felt an absurd, headstrong desire to put an arm around her shoulders, as if to envelop her, drag her into his secret world. He managed to restrain the actual gesture, yet he had the strange impression that he had made it, so that now when he caught her eye he smiled meaningfully. It seemed to him that her smile in response was almost as from one who had in fact shared some secret.

What she said in fact, was, 'It's suddenly quite cold, isn't it?'

He moved quickly. 'I'll shut the window.'

She smiled her gratitude, and he pulled the window firmly shut. As he did so it occurred to him with wonder that they were all at once like two creatures caught up in a self-created cocoon. He looked back and could just make out the heads of the others spread out on the rear deck: May and Alan in one corner, Di and Ted in the other. They were obviously watching the rise and fall of the boat, engrossed, caught up in their little worlds.

He turned and looked at Merle beside him. She appeared detached, spiritually and physically apart, almost like an object of flawless beauty. He stared, indulging for once in the sheer sensual pleasure of observing such beauty.

Suddenly, before he could compose himself, she looked up and caught his eye. He felt like a man caught in the act of some crime, of stealing perhaps, or worse. Yet he could not look away, even though he felt a faint flush on his cheeks. He could not be sure what she thought or felt, but after a moment or two he saw a faint smile lingering at her lips, which all at once had acquired a deepening colour. And then, very quietly, she put her hand up on the wheel and rested it on his, sleek and soft to the touch – and now, he noticed, quite warm.

At Salcombe there was a bar across the entrance to the estuary and Ted took control until they were safely past. Then he handed the wheel back to Max in order to concentrate on the task of getting ready the huge fisherman anchor at the prow of the boat.

'Hasn't been used for God knows how long,' swore Ted, struggling away. Now, out of the surge of the sea and in the calm of the blue estuary, with the afternoon sunshine blazing down, it was suddenly very hot. Ted had already taken off his thick fisherman's jersey: now, swearing at the recalcitrant anchor, he paused and pulled off his shirt. He seemed happier working in the freedom of being stripped to the waist and, straining and heaving, managed to lift the enormous anchor onto the edge. For a man of his age he appeared to have kept himself remarkably lithe and fit; as he worked his muscles rippled under skin that was smooth and brown from years of living under the hot sun.

After a while, finding the anchor too much weight, Ted called Alan over. The younger man was altogether less agile and adept, but between them they got the anchor up on the side. There Ted paused, standing with an easy rather attractive indolence, while slowly Max steered the boat up the channel.

'Take it easy. We've a little way yet.'

Max concentrated on steering while the others relaxed. Di, who had been watching the anchoring operations with a shrewd eye, now moved over to where Ted was standing, looking a little like some swashbuckling pirate of old. Through the window Max heard her teasing him lightly.

'I see you're a good customer for the tattooist. How many times have you been tattooed, Ted?'

Ted laughed, unconsciously expanding his massive chest so that the blue curling marks showed up more clearly. From where Max was it was difficult to see them precisely, but it looked like the conventional tattoo marks of snakes and serpents. Also one or two names, which he could not read.

Di raised a finger and began tracing out the spelling.

'Rose ... Marie ... June ... I'm surprised at you, Ted!'

The big skipper grinned down at Di, whose finger went on vaguely tracing the letterings.

'A girl in every port, that's what you had, I'll bet,' said Di almost angrily.

Watching idly out of the wheelhouse window, it occurred to

Max that the contrast between the two of them was almost ludicrous. Ted was six feet tall at least, and beside him Di seemed a minute creature, sturdy indeed but short. Yet somehow, in an odd way, he could almost comprehend the underlying pull between the two of them, the long and the short, the big and small; once, indeed, Ted almost made an instinctive movement as if to encompass within his powerful hands the petite figure beside him.

At last, as if feeling the necessity of breaking some strange spell, Max called out.

'Is this where you want to anchor?'

Ted looked around quickly, Di quite forgotten.

'Yes, this will do fine. Shut down the engine, hold her there. Now come on, you lubbers, over with the anchor.'

It worked simply enough. The great anchor clattered down and held firm, and they were snugly fixed for the night. A beautiful night it was, too. They rowed the dinghy to the quayside and wandered through the town, eating a meal in a restaurant by the waterside. Alan and May got a little drunk, unusual for them, and on the way back they linked arms and danced from side to side of the road in curious, obstinate rhythms, so that the others had to keep avoiding the lumbering figures.

'Steady there,' said Ted, but jovially. He walked along one side of Di, Max on the other. Merle trailed a little behind, inhaling the soft night air gently.

After a while Max dropped back.

'Dreaming again?'

'Mmmmmmmm. It's a night for dreaming, isn't it?'

This was true enough. A big silver moon hung low over the bay, colouring everything with a misty glow so that nothing looked quite real. On such a night, thought Max, on such a night.

'When I get back I think I'll take a midnight swim,' said Merle almost to herself, so low that no one except Max heard her.

They rowed back noisily, May and Alan clinging together and attempting unsuccessfully to sing bawdy songs. Max did not know whether to be annoyed or amused. He had the feeling that in some surprising way they were discovering their secret lives for the first time.

Back on the boat Alan and May disappeared drunkenly to their cabin, waving hearty goodbyes. Once they had closed the door behind them there was a sudden, almost physical silence. Max followed Di and Ted down into the tiny saloon, and sat there while Di made a quick cup of tea. Somehow, over the tea, Ted started talking, and soon was immersing himself in endless recollections of his sea days. Another time Max might have listened with the same fascination that he saw registered on Di's face as she sat curled up in a corner seat, her eyes fixed almost avidly on Ted's expressive face. Some other night, perhaps; but not this night.

At an opportune moment he slipped to the deck. All was strangely still. The shore had faded away into the shimmering background, and nothing seemed alive except the rippling water and, overhead, the huge hanging moon.

Suddenly his straining ears caught a faint slithering sound, such as a fish might make in the water. He went quietly round to the moonlit stern of the boat and was just in time to make out a shadow flitting across the water. He called out softly:

'Merle …'

There was no answer, and he could not really know whether she had heard him or not. Or perhaps, he thought wryly as he quickly slipped off his clothes, perhaps it wasn't Merle but some kind of mermaid.

The water, as he slipped noiselessly into it, was quite warm, enveloping him caressingly. He pushed off from the boat and struck away down the moonlit avenue, meantime looking from right to left with each overarm stroke.

At first he could not see her.

'Merle, where are you?'

And then, magically, even like a mermaid, she frothed up in the water almost at his side, her long hair dank and wound round her neck, her eyes brighter than ever in the moonlight.

'Isn't it lovely?'

'Yes,' he murmured. 'Lovely.'

She grinned at him with curious insolence, like a naughty child, then splashed water in his face and with a gurgle turned and swam away.

'Catch me if you can!'

He struck out after the elusive girl, swimming with powerful strokes. But she was a good swimmer, too, and she played him a mischievous hide-and-seek in the shimmering moon-blessed night. At last with a spurt he reached out and clasped the disappearing curve of her shoulder, holding on as if for life itself, until with a gurgle of laughter she turned and, like him, trod water.

'Merle,' he said, suddenly afraid now that it was too late. Beneath his hand he felt the quiver of the flesh that he had never known, never really thought about, now sensually entwined with his own in the cool water. He was terribly, achingly conscious of her whole being a few inches away. Slowly he pulled her towards him.

She did not resist. It was almost, he reflected later, as if she had been expecting the moment, had even wanted it. He felt her come up to him, almost with familiarity, the softness of her limbs inexplicably melting into his own. It was a unique enough experience, the embrace in the sea, yet he could not help feeling it was even more unique, that she and perhaps even he, too, belonged momentarily to some other, less earthly plane.

He kissed her gently yet sensually, before the rising water forced them to break the embrace and keep themselves afloat. Then as they swam together again he touched her face, her neck, her shoulders, pulled gently, teasingly, at her long tresses.

'My mermaid.' And then, more troubledly, 'Oh, Merle.'

It was her turn suddenly not to speak, as they swam around that one, magical spot where they had met for the first time. And all at once he comprehended that there was nothing more to say, nothing more that dared to be said. The only peace left on earth was to swim gently round and round, their white, innocent bodies momentarily at one with all the other fishes of the sea.

Just once more, when they had swum up to the boat and were holding on to the side, he drew her to him. This time there was nothing to impede their embrace, which was somehow still part of the night and yet also, tremulously, of some unknown future.

Then she wriggled out of his arms and silently climbed up onto the boat. His last glimpse was of a white shadow melting into nothingness. By the time, suddenly weary, he climbed aboard, he was all alone again.

He picked up his clothes and crept down to his darkened cabin. He climbed into bed silently, pulling himself deep down into the clothes. Only gradually, listening for sounds, did he become aware that Di had not yet come to bed. He tried to imagine her closeted below with Ted, listening to those sea stories, perhaps losing herself in quite a different, more earthy world. But somehow his mind was too tired to conjure up the possibilities. Slowly he began to drop off to sleep and was too tired to awaken when finally, an hour later, she came to bed. He stirred just once, a little later, and heard the even sound of her breathing, and began to wonder if the evening, which seemed over, might ever really end.

The next day, early, they headed out of Salcombe bound for Falmouth and the end of the trip. If was a curious, different day. All at once the rough weather had vanished with the western winds; the sea, if not as smooth as the proverbial sheet of glass, was very comfortable. Max held the steering wheel easily and lightly and the boat's bow rose and fell with a pleasant, easy, rhythmic movement.

'Just think,' he said, half complainingly. 'It might have been like this all the way.'

Beside him, twiddling the knobs of the radio, Ted said over his shoulder:

'You should be glad really. It's given you a chance to really know your ship. Now you won't be afraid of any kind of weather.'

Max thought, surprised, *he's right, too*. He felt a great surge of confidence in the boat. He fixed his eye on the horizon, looking for the needle point of Eddystone lighthouse.

'There she blows!' called out Ted, jovially, always keener-eyed than anyone. 'About five degrees to starboard and then hold her on that course.'

Obediently Max corrected the wheel, still staring ahead. It gave him a sweet satisfaction to be solely in charge of the boat, taking her with him over the unknown horizon. He stared over to where the thin line of the lighthouse gradually took shape, like some ghost suddenly made real perhaps by an act of faith.

'Good morning,' said a faint voice – no, two faint voices – at his side. He looked round and smiled faintly at Alan and May.

'Hullo. Got a hangover?'

They nodded sheepishly.

'Well,' he began, and then broke off, smiling again. He could not help eyeing them shrewdly, trying to contemplate their night together. He had a fleeting, inspired image of their two bodies stirring in the night, turning to one another hungrily, as if they had never before felt quite such desperation.

He ran a tongue over his lips nervously, aware of his confusion. He looked through the rear window of the wheelhouse to where Di and Merle were both sunbathing on the stern roof. They were lying full length on their stomachs and all he could see was the same soft expanse of arched, sunning backs, the flurry of Di's blonde hair, the deep darkness of Merle's.

He turned away, still confused, glad to feel the steady, controlled rhythm of the boat whose fate he guided.

Ted came in from checking up on the ropes. His lined face looked, somehow, more youthful than before.

'Well, won't be long now.'

'Are you glad?' said Max, curious.

Ted shrugged.

'All trips have to end.' He shrugged again, as if in some way to convince himself. 'It's a job.'

They both stared ahead, looking for the rise of land that would give them a fix on the entrance to Falmouth. At last Max spied it, remembering the hilltop from rambles of childhood days.

'You're right,' conceded Ted. 'Good work.'

Ted took over the wheel and Max went out on the front deck. After a while the others came and joined him. Alan and May, holding hands in some strange protective way, leaned over the port rail, watching the waves gently gliding by. As if at a signal both Di and Merle came along the deck, stretching themselves after their sleep.

'We're coming into port,' Max said. He looked at Di,

pleased at the eagerness on her face. He bent forward.

'Well, are you pleased with the boat?'

Di looked up at him, her blue eyes clear and unconfused. He was surprised to read in them an unexpected warmth – affection, too.

'Of course I am. It's been wonderful, the whole trip.'

She went forward to the very tip of the boat, spreading herself like some figurehead of old over the prow. Indeed he thought, in some subtle way she welded into the view, as if all the latent power gathered into her small, compact form was splayed out in a spray of energy that carried the boat forward even faster.

He was conscious of Merle standing to one side of him, clothed, correct, as distant as perhaps she had ever been. He wondered what she was thinking, guessed her thoughts to be as confused as his own. How could anything be the same again?

They rounded the black and white lump of St Anthony Lights, and there before them stretched the magnificence of the Carrick Roads, with the docks of Falmouth on one side and the continental colours of the houses of St Mawes on the other.

Above him Max was conscious of Ted bringing the wheel over to port, heading them down the inner channel, past the big stone parapets of the first dock and towards Falmouth town. He heard the window open and Ted leaned out above him, calling out.

'Now don't forget, the mooring buoy is a small red one. I'll bring the boat up very slowly and then I want to pick that up and pull the chain aboard, then we're anchored.' There was a pause, and then Ted repeated the words more slowly and added almost as an afterthought.

'There's no need to worry, it's all quite simple – all we've got to do is to pick up our mooring and we're home.'

Slowly the powerful diesel engine took the boat further into the sheltering confines of Falmouth harbour. They stood in their own little citadels on the long green sea-washed deck, alone with their momentary thoughts. At last the little red buoy was sighted, bobbing up and down, awaiting their claim. Slowly, relentlessly, like time itself, they edged towards it. At last Max leaned over, boat hook in hand. For a passing moment he thought, *I might easily miss it, we would sail on and on*

... But bending forward, quite expertly, he managed to grip the buoy and quickly pull up the chain. Ted came running out of the wheelhouse to help him. Moments later they had the chain in fast, and the boat was finally moored.

Suddenly, quite emotionally drained, Max went and leaned against the wheelhouse door, looking out upon the lush beauty of the huge harbour, the smooth blue surface sprinkled colourfully with all kinds of boats, yachts and sloops and yawls and cutters and schooners and tugs and motor boats. In the background, like a frame to the picture, bloomed the high spring colours of the fields above Flushing. It was a lovely, enduring spring afternoon scene.

Well, he thought, *that's that. The trip is over.* And then, catching a caustic glance from Di up at the front, sensing the dark shadow of Merle moving behind, he contemplated uneasily the other voyage that was only beginning – and this one without any charts, and a fair chance of being wrecked.

V

Memories of Michaelmas House

Michaelmas House stands somewhere along the edge of Hampstead Heath, with an impressive view over London rooftops to the dusty dome of St Paul's – one of a row of large, rambling and rather decrepit houses that cling desperately to the remnants of their nineteenth century grandeur. Why it was called Michaelmas House I never found out, but I remember my first impression was that of something approaching a slumbering ruin, rather than of the more cheerful abode suggested by the name. Grey austere walls broken here and there by grimy windows from which most of the surrounding paint had peeled away; a tattered trellis porch leading to a cumbersome front doorway whose panels of coloured glass were covered with innumerable cracks and splinters; a garden that, apart from an unfinished artificial rockery, stretched away into hopeless tangles of undergrowth – the whole rounded off in character by a dismal and peeling signboard that creaked with every waft of the breeze, reading: PRIVATE BOARDING ESTABLISHMENT. And yet it was a misleading impression for inside the house, so far as was humanly possible within the limits imposed by early nineteenth century architecture, there was (during my stay there early in the war) an abundance of colour, life and excitement. I should like, while imagination is still unrationed, to recapture a few of my more vivid memories of Michaelmas House and its residents.

Our landlord, and to some extent the focal point of the house, was Jonathan Johns, a small, shrivelled, but lively old man whose bright bald head contrasted strangely with the fact that the rest of his face was immersed behind thick white side-whiskers, culminating in a straggling beard. When I first saw him, and on most occasions, he wore a bulging check sports-coat, blue corduroy trousers, and his feet shuffled along in red carpet slippers that positively screamed out. A pair of horn-rimmed pince-nez, which he was always losing, gave him an owlish and rather dreamy look, but in fact he was an extremely wide-awake old man, though perhaps not exactly the type one would expect to be landlord of a London boarding house. He had, as it happened, spent practically the whole of his lifetime as curator to a large museum, retiring some years previously to devote himself to a life of leisure and reading. Unfortunately for him his sister, who it was intended should administer to his bodily comforts, died soon after her money had enabled them to acquire Michaelmas House, and Jonathan found himself a solitary occupant, faced with considerable difficulties in obtaining paid help of any permanency. Applying his natural cunning to the problem, he hit on the idea of advertising the house as a boarding establishment, thus enticing in sundry people from among whom he could somehow obtain a little housewifely attention and, particularly, a supply of regular meals. It was an idea, moreover, that worked exceedingly well for, although boarders came and went quite continuously, there were invariably two or three feminine residents upon whom the carefully practised charms of an elderly gentleman could work wonders.

Jonathan was a dilatory landlord, seldom showing any interest in the material comfort of his boarders, meeting all complaints with a bland and deceitful assurance that something would be done as soon as possible. At the same time he was very much a part of everyone's daily life for the simple reason that, all other accommodation being filled, he himself had been forced to make a home in the large entrance hall – into the centre of which emerged the only staircase in the house. Thus, to come in or go out of the house, as well as to reach the only kitchen and the back-garden, we all had to use the same intrusive route. Far from Jonathan showing any signs of embarrassment it was usually the boarder who suffered. For our landlord was a painstaking student of human nature, and during each passage through his room one felt a pair of beady and observant eyes studying every movement. It was, in fact, quite impossible to hide from Jonathan, anything but the most intimate secrets – and very often these, too, were spotted.

Moreover, having observed, Jonathan could seldom restrain himself from imparting the results of his observations – which usually meant that journeys through his room had to be broken awhile to hear the latest sly piece of gossip. This was really the reason why so many people, with every apparent attention of settling into Michaelmas House, suddenly and wrathfully took themselves off elsewhere. I think, on the whole, most of us rather enjoyed it – though none so much as Jonathan. I can see him now, sitting up in bed in the morning, chattering gaily to the two or three boarders who were awaiting their turn to make their breakfast in the kitchen – looking, with his pink bedcap and his flowing beard, not unlike a modern Methuselah. Perhaps it is needless to add that, although Jonathan sat up in bed, he seldom did so until he was quite certain that a soft-hearted boarder had begun to prepare him a cup of tea and some toast. In return for this service Jonathan would regale his enforced visitors with opinions and assertions on a hundred-and-one subjects with which he had made himself theoretically acquainted during long sojourns in his museum. In fact, Jonathan believed in the theoretical approach to life to such an extent that never once during my stay did I ever see him do a stroke of physical work – although of course, this might have been due, as he would assert, to his forgetfulness. It was one of the old man's proudest moments when he finally evolved what he claimed to be a foolproof system of jogging his errant memory. Under this he kept a large store of paperslips and wrote down on a separate slip any item which he wished to keep in mind. Usually there were thirty or forty slips, which meant he had to spend at least an hour every morning sorting them out in order of importance. Often there was never time, in a life of such leisured pace as Jonathan's, to deal with more than two or three in a day. Still he seemed to think it such an ingenious system that he often talked about making it the subject of a book. Later on he developed it further by making a habit, just before going to bed, of writing on a large sheet of paper: NAME, Jonathan Johns, AGE, 71 years, nine months, fifteen days, TO-MORROW IS – TO-MORROW'S TASKS ARE – He said that otherwise he was afraid he might wake up in the morning and have no idea of who he was or where he was or what he was supposed to do.

Athough Jonathan was our official landlord, he was, during my stay at least, not undisputedly so. It was impossible to get to the bottom of the disagreement, but it appeared that, possibly in a moment of financial despondency, Jonathan once advertised Michaelmas House for sale, in rather fanciful terms. A Mr and Mrs Peacock, then running a genteel country house on the Suffolk coast – plunged into gloom and emptiness by war conditions – wrote eagerly and anxiously, making a tempting offer. Jonathan, being Jonathan, asked for a fairly large deposit, cashed the cheque, and then decided to stay on, talking vaguely about 'waiting till things clarified.' At last, in despair, the Peacocks disposed of their guest house to the War Office and embarked for London. They turned up one day at Michaelmas House without any warning, accompanied by large amounts of furniture and luggage, not to mention their fifteen-year-old daughter, Paula, product of an obscure progressive school. Jonathan resolutely refused to renounce his proprietorship, but the Peacocks, by a tremendous effort of nervous energy, managed to get themselves established on the ground floor. Being in reality a shy and diffident couple, they then relapsed into a period of inactivity. Every now and then Mrs Peacock, a buxom and kindly lady who belonged irrevocably to Leamington Spa or Bath, would corner Jonathan and talk to him gravely about honourable agreements, and arrangements between gentlemen. Somehow Jonathan always managed to get away with things left indecisive. A more aggressive couple than the Peacocks might have got in lawyers and solicitors and so on. After a time it became obviously too late for this, and they seemed to settle down into a patient existence lightened merely by some far-away spark of hope, an airy assurance by Jonathan that they should have first option on the house as soon as he was able to leave. In the meantime it was mutually agreed that Mrs Peacock – who possibly wished to keep her genteel hostess touch – could take in a boarder during the long months when her daughter was away at school. Thus there developed within Michaelmas House a tiny inner establishment, subtly removed from the rest of the house, where the Peacocks delicately entertained a series of quiet elderly ladies and Civil Servants. Mrs Peacock's husband had little to do with all this; being a dreamy and unworldly person who spent the larger part of his time painting views of Hampstead Heath. He brought with him several large boxes full of mounted paintings, and these were exhibited over every available piece of space in the Peacocks' ground-floor rooms. A sight of the paintings might have inclined the view that theirs was definitely a minority appeal, but in fact we learnt that Mr Peacock earned quite a fair income from them. The reason for this was that each of the series of boarders so genteelly cared for by Mrs Peacock invariably felt (or was made to feel) conscience-bound to purchase at least one painting. Apparently in their country guest house there had been a Peacock painting in each of the eighteen bedrooms and quite a roaring trade had been done.

It was Mr and Mrs Peacock's united hope that their daughter Paula would follow in her father's footsteps, if perhaps a little more successfully, but this was a hope unlikely, the rest of us felt, to be fulfilled. We were once given a view of a curious blotch of colours representing Paula's first attempt at painting, but far the greater part of the young lady's time and undoubtedly all her creative talent and energy went – during her stays in Michaelmas House – into initiating the most alarming upheavals and disasters. The period of Paula Peacock's holidays was of tense preparation on the part of other residents. Rooms were locked, articles capable of damage were secreted in the most unlikely places, while actual personal contact was avoided as far as possible. This procedure was more than justified, for Paula's progressive school was one of those places which encouraged complete freedom from inhibitions. If Paula wished to run up to someone and kick them on the shin, Paula should be encouraged not only to do so but to repeat the performance as much as she desired, without any uneducative hindrance from the person concerned. If Paula felt a desire to break a window, or several windows – if Paula wished to pour treacle over the keys of a typewriter – if Paula wished to disintegrate a few articles of furniture or perhaps start a bonfire of the curtains – if Paula wished to parade in the street outside in a state of nudity – if Paula, in fact, wished to stand on her head – on no account was she to be prevented. The effect of all this can perhaps be imagined: it was worst of all upon Jonathan, whom this creature (described quite seriously by Mrs Peacock as a 'charming little girl') made the subject of her most frightening schemes. Whether this behaviour was cunningly, if not openly, encouraged by her parents we could never decide. Perhaps there was sometimes an element of sadistic enjoyment on our own part, even as we deprecated little incidents such as the setting fire to Jonathan's beard while he slept, the wilful scattering across Hampstead Heath of piles of memory slips, and so on. But this was merely the despicable attitude of those who know that another's suffering means a respite to their own.

Perhaps by reason of age and geographical position Jonathan seemed to me to dominate the complex family of human beings making up Michaelmas House. Yet I have striking memories of some of my fellow boarders. Professor Samson was the next oldest inhabitant to Jonathan, although a very different character. Where Jonathan was bold and colourful and dramatic, the Professor was mild and meek and effacing. As a personality, that is – in his profession of inventor, which he followed with a fervour that is indescribable, he could in fact be as much a terrorising influence on the life of Michaelmas House as Paula Peacock. His room, tucked away in a high corner of the house, was a reflection of his vast interests and intentions. The walls were lined with avenues of austere tomes, under their various labels: ANTHROPOLOGICAL, BIO-CHEMICAL, DYNAMO-ELECTRICAL, HYDRO-THERAPEUTICAL, SOCIOLOGICAL, etc. The room was invariably in a state of chaos – stacks of bound copies of scientific journals, a tumbledown writing desk piled high with papers, a work-bench strewn with tools, bottles, tins of nuts and bolts – ending dramatically with a large lathe into which a steel rod was usually fixed at such an angle that it jutted out and filled the way of passage. The Professor spared little thought for anything but his work, and indeed literally lived and slept among it. His bed ran alongside his working bench; the old armchair in which he presumably occasionally relaxed was usually piled high with precision instruments; the table on which he kept many of his chemicals was also his dining-table. Here and there dotted about among the bottles one might come across a plate of moulding cheese, a half-used loaf, a raw onion, a bowl of cold soup, a bone of meat, a can of beans, of spaghetti, of spam – all spread over an incredibly lifeless tea-cloth which, like most of the objects, might remain on the table for months on end.

During the whole of my stay I never discovered any conclusive results to the Professor's experiments, although – with his flowing hair, his bushy eyebrows and his gaunt, stooping body, he had all the appearance of a man of imponderable genius. He was always anxious to persuade people to make use of his inventions. As soon as I moved in he came round and insisted on presenting me with a pot of dark evil-looking paint with which to paint the walls of my room. He advised me to give the walls a thorough coating, after which, he said, they would not need touching for another twenty-five years, owing to some long-wearing property he had introduced into the mixture. I was foolish enough to follow his advice and discovered that, no doubt due to an oversight on the inventor's part, the paint possessed no heat resistance, so that as soon as the electric light was turned on in the evening great rivers of coloured liquid began streaming down the walls. In the end I had to spend a day washing the walls and recovering them with a pot of paint bought at Woolworth's. A number of the Professor's inventions were installed in the kitchen – including an air-blower which one worked with the foot, like the blower of an organ, meanwhile holding washed plates in front to dry; a small flute-like gadget which, when fixed to the spout of the kettle, played the opening notes of 'God Save the King' as soon as the water was boiling; a bread-cutting machine which no one ever dared to use. Other inventions extended all over the house – one of the most ambitious being an extra-widened piping system which ran through every room and was fitted with convenient flapdoors. The idea was that anyone in his or her room who wished to dispose of dirty water merely opened the flap and poured it away, to drain out in the proper quarters. Unfortunately constant sluicing of a variety of mixtures resulted in the pipes becoming blocked, so that liquid on being poured in, would as like as not spurt out again. Alternatively the pressure might send a stream of dirty liquid splashing out in someone else's room, and there would inevitably ensue one of those household eruptions with which I learned to become familiar at Michaelmas House. One other ambitious application of the Professor's inventive mind took the form of a complete electrical wiring of the house, reaching to the roof, where the wires were connected at regular intervals with flammable fuses. This was the Samson 'Air Raid Precaution System', so designed that if fire-bombs should fall on the roof the heat would melt the fuses, thus setting off a series of tiny bells that were fixed in residents' bedrooms. As it happened, fire-bombs never actually fell on the roof, but during the hottest period of the summer several false, and somewhat confusing alarms were caused through the fuses being melted by the sun. On one occasion it took a period of three hours and the services of an electrical engineer to stop the bells ringing.

Another resident I remember with particular affection was Miss Nelson, the school-teacher, in many ways the most adventurous of all the residents, despite her forty odd years. A tiny bright-eyed woman, full of a cheerful pixie-like friendliness, she was forever acquiring – and as suddenly dropping – new enthusiasms. I think it was because she inevitably attempted to force these enthusiasms upon whatever pupils she happened to be teaching that Miss Nelson had never risen very high in her profession – although she did not seem to bear any resentment about this. When I arrived at Michaelmas House Miss Nelson's current enthusiasm was folk-dancing. After reading all the available literature she bought some folk-dance music on gramophone records and, one summer evening, proceeded to give an exhibition of folk-dancing in the back garden. She was dressed in a loose and extremely short costume of the sort peculiarly suitable only for young schoolchildren, and she wore a large blue bow in her hair. No doubt this was the correct costume, but taken together with the fact that Miss Nelson's pert face was over-awed by a pair of horn-rimmed glasses, plus the discovery that she was bow-legged, it was inevitable that our attention should be distracted from a proper aesthetic appreciation. Perhaps Miss Nelson felt this: at any rate it was her first and last performance. She attempted in turn basketware, needlework, vase decoration and toy making, producing in each case an example with which she herself seemed to be eminently satisfied, but about which there was always a curious air of inconclusiveness. She insisted on presenting each work for the use of the house. In most cases it was found possible, judiciously, to misplace these items, but not so in the case of Miss Nelson's greatest achievement, a hand-made wicker chair. This had to occupy a permanent position of importance in the garden, and out of implicit politeness we used to take turns in somehow inserting ourselves into it – until, one day, the thing disintegrated under the fifteen-and-a-half stone pressure of Mr Brabazon from the top floor. Miss Nelson had subsequent phases of interest in poetry reading, dress reform, amateur dramatics and Ancient Greek. Her most alarming period, however, was when she developed a conviction that she had a peculiar, and indeed unique, affinity with animals. It began one day when she was found crouching on the staircase nursing a huge Persian cat and muttering into its ear. When I asked her, half-jokingly, if she were talking to it in baby-language, she looked at me with obvious impatience and said abruptly: 'Not at all, I'm talking in *pussy* language.' For a short time Miss Nelson went around fondling and making advances to various pets in the immediate vicinity, until neighbours began to complain and threaten to report her to the police. This decided her that she must possess some animals of her own, but her peculiar inability successfully to conclude any project prevented her from simply acquiring a cat, or a dog, or even a parrot. After some frantic journeying about London, she turned up flourishing a suitcase in which, wrapped in an old bonnet, were two day-old chicks. For a time these delightful little things brought out all the maternal in Miss Nelson. She carried them about with her wherever she went; usually, for want of anywhere else in a tiny shopping basket, but on rare occasions – having apparently read about it in a book – amid the unkempt strands of her hair, where the chicks seemed so happy that they frequently burst into song. One would like to be able to record that Miss Nelson mothered and reared the chicks as her own children – or at least that she obtained some practical return from them in the form of eggs. The sad truth is that in time Miss Nelson lost interest in her chicks (as she did in most things) and gave them away to Mrs Capek, a Czech refugee with a sense of practical values, who presented Mr Capek, that evening, with roast chicken.

On the same floor as Miss Nelson, but in much stricter seclusion, there lived a Russian named Turkovitch, who claimed to be one of the only two representatives in the whole of England of a certain variety of the Ukrainian peoples (the other lived in Aberdeen and they carried on a continuous and furious correspondence). For the most part Turkovitch remained a dark, morose and solitary man, but there were occasions when, in a fit of that extravagant jubilation peculiar to the Russian temperament, he would bring home bottles of imitation vodka, get drunk, and appear impressively at the head of the staircase, clad in a magnificent Cossack hat and a startling, though frayed, uniform of the Czar's Army. Sometimes, he would give uninvited renderings of obscure Russian songs, inviting all and sundry to join in, but we were always held back by an uneasy feeling that we were enacting a scene from one of the older Russian comedies. Turkovitch always carried under his arm thick dossiers of important-looking papers; this, and the fact that he was to be heard at all hours of the night hammering at his typewriter encouraged an impression that he was mixed up in high and revolutionary politics. Now and then he was reported to have been seen sitting among a group of sinister-looking men in Lyons' Corner House. But as a rule Turkovitch managed to shroud all his activities with a cloak of mystery and secrecy. This inclination was responsible for one dramatic gesture that endeared him to most of us – a blank refusal to make use of the over-public staircase of Michaelmas House. Somehow he procured a ladder and for many weeks used to climb in and out of his window and up and down the ladder. As he was constantly forgetting to put away the ladder many unfortunate passers-by fell over it, and in the end the police registered a complaint. However, the final solution – his transference to a room on the ground-floor where he was able, with comparative ease, to climb in and out of his window on to terra firma – undoubtedly left the victory with Turkovitch.

Then there was Edgar. From the fair curly top of his head to the shining soles of his sandalled-feet, Edgar exuded hearty health. He was at least six feet three inches tall, with a strapping, brawny, if somewhat ungainly, body – a body which was constantly being thrust forward, almost aggressively, as if

to say – look, here, don't you wish I belonged to you? Even on
the coldest day, Edgar's huge area of muscular flesh was
seldom protected by more than a short-sleeved shirt, wide and
defiantly open at the neck, and a pair of khaki shorts. When
not at his job as a physical training instructor he was usually in
the garden at Michaelmas House – running, jumping, leaping,
bending, flinging himself on to the ground and then into the
air, performing quite incredible physical exercises and turning
frequent somersaults. Edgar's whole life had been changed
through reading a book, by a health expert called Dr
Hasselfisch. The main message of the book was that it was up
to everyone, if they wished to be healthy, to embark on a
'Period of Rejuvenation'. This consisted in complete
abstention from food for three weeks, accompanied by daily
walks of at least ten miles, a series of strenuous exercises, and
constant cold baths. Edgar underwent two 'Periods of
Rejuvenation' during my stay. On each occasion he ended up
by collapsing and having to stay in bed for several days, but he
re-emerged pronouncing, to our despair, and despite great
hollow rings around his eyes, that he never felt better in his life
... To express his philosophy concisely Edgar was fond of
coining slogans, and decorated his rooms with several – Health
Before Wealth, You are Your Best Doctor, Treasure your
Greatest Treasure – Your Body, and so on. It was part of the
Hasselfisch system, religiously observed by Edgar, to eat tiny
meals of bread-and-cheese and lettuce at three-hourly
intervals throughout the day. Once every hour, no matter
where he was, Edgar had to lie down and relax for ten minutes.
First thing in the morning it was Doctor Hasselfisch's insistent
desire that Edgar should go out into the garden and, in a state
of nakedness, perform deep breathing exercises followed by
sunbathing. Often there was no sun and quite a cool wind, but
Edgar believed in sticking to the letter of the law and laid
himself down faithfully. We discovered one useful attribute of
Edgar's. If he was accosted with anything remotely resembling
a challenge to, or reflecting upon, his physical capacities – such
as 'I'll bet you couldn't dig that vegetable bed in
half-an-hour!' – he would immediately take up the challenge
and prove his prowess. In this way we got many odd jobs done
about the house that might otherwise have been neglected.

Another visitor from overseas that made Michaelmas House his temporary home was Singh, a quiet suave Indian student with large mournful eyes, brimming over with their untold suffering. He had a curious capacity for hovering in the background of a room so that one was hardly aware of his presence. Singh could tell the most colourful stories of his life out in India, as the son of a phenomenally rich Rajah, but invariably he would end by requesting the loan of five shillings. He filled up his days with an intricate series of carefully studied actions – a gentle stroll around the West End, an afternoon at the pictures, an evening reclining on someone's couch listening to the pleasant sound of his own voice. It was the female sex, however, in which Singh was principally interested, in a sad, wistful and generally frustrated way. Whenever a new female resident arrived at Michaelmas House Singh would blossom out into an attendant and charming cavalier, finally inviting the young lady up to his room to see his Indian paintings. Singh may have had some Indian paintings, but inevitably after one of these occasions he would relapse back into his slumbering life and the young lady would go about with her head high in the air for a few days.

And so the memories flow by. Miriam and Molly, the two hard-boiled Communist adherents who stuck pamphlets by Harry Pollitt in the lavatories and incited rebellion; the one and only maidservant that Jonathan was ever able to obtain; Mr Brabazon, large and rotund, well-dressed, his pocket always full of the best brands of cigars, who followed the curiously ethereal profession of preaching an obscure philosophy of Yogi-ism, with such success that before the war he hired the Albert Hall; Marigold, the exquisitely cool and self-controlled chorus girl who carried her cold loveliness in and out of our lives without any of us ever really finding out whether she was made of flesh or marble; Mrs Strutt, another of the stately breed, who had triumphantly spent her life outliving the members of a large and widespread family, and kept the most detailed records of the exact place and nature of their diseases and deaths. One of the last new residents during my stay – and certainly the shortest-lived – was a member of a travelling circus. He was a likable Swede, whose life had been full of all sorts of hair-raising adventures, but he omitted to mention, until he was installed, that his particular profession was that of a guardian of a troupe of three performing seals – and wherever he went the seals had to go. For some days on end the seals lived in comparative luxury in our only bathroom but in the end, after they had embarked on a nocturnal Cook's tour of various bedrooms, the whole of the residents of Michaelmas House united, for probably the first and last time, in a protest meeting, and the Swede, in something of a huff, was sent to find another home for himself and his seals.

That is how I remember life at Michaelmas House – a series of undulating excitements and events, an ebb and flow of odd, perverse, but somehow alive people. In these days when the world is rapidly assuming a state of highly-disciplined uniformity it would be nice to think of Michaelmas House remaining as a defiant tower of perverse individualism. But alas! – it has already been commandeered by some eagle-eyed planning expert and converted into what must be a rather impracticable nursery for the offspring of women factory workers. New brooms will have swept, the place will be alive with the fresh laughter of children, and quite right too … But I wouldn't be surprised, should I ever peep in, if I saw a few jovial ghosts gambolling in some forgotten corner.

VI

The Day the Car Fell in the Harbour

Sammy Richards is a great friend of mine, kind-hearted and ever ready to do a good turn, but at the same time, with a true Cornishman's shrewdness and sharp eye for business. That was why, after a visitor's car had accidentally gone over the quayside here in our little Cornish holiday town, Sammy was quick on the spot, as befitting our local garage man, to offer the shaken owner ten pounds cash for the remains of his bedraggled car.

At first, the owner said he'd think about it, and went off home to recover. But the next morning he rang up to say 'Yes,' and so Sammy posted off his cheque for ten pounds, and presumably thought with some satisfaction, that was that.

The very next day I came across him, looking slyly pleased with himself.

'C'm'n have a drink,' he said jovially, 'while Sammy tells you how to do big business.'

As soon as he had posted his cheque, it appeared, he had simply made a telephone call to Harry Tregenza's scrapyard, at Porthtreen, and Harry had agreed to take the car for fifteen pounds.

'Harry,' Sammy had said, gratefully, 'for fifteen pounds I'll tow her straight over to you, here and now.'

He downed his drink with satisfaction.

'Which is just what I did, and here I am with five pounds profit, and well rid of that dying duck.'

Alas, poor Sammy, as the old saying goes, it never does to count your chickens ... etc ...

The next morning I came across him, looking pale and jittery.

'What do you think? What *do* you think? You know I sold

that car to Harry Tregenza? Well, this morning, if you please, that ... Mr Smith sends back my ten-pound cheque and says he never gave any written permission to sell the car, and he's changed his mind, and has decided to keep it, and will I please arrange to have it transported to London. Would you believe it, now?

Sammy held his hands to his head and rocked from side to side.

'That car ... I wish I'd left it there in the harbour.'

'Never mind,' I said, soothingly. 'It's only a day since you took it over to Harry Tregenza. Let's drive over now and buy it back.'

We drove over in grim silence, the gloom only lifting as we pulled in at the scrapyard and saw the grey saloon standing in one corner. We got out and hurried over to it, Sammy touching the body almost lovingly.

'There you are, my sweetheart. For a moment I was afraid ...'

Suddenly, his whole being stiffened in what I abruptly gathered was horror. Then, with an exclamation, he lifted up the bonnet and poked his head inside.

'What's the matter?' I said.

Sammy held the bonnet high and beckoned me closer.

'That's what's the matter, me cock sparrer. Just that. A slight case, you might say, of something missing.'

In fact, the grey saloon no longer had an engine at all.

Harry Tregenza was most apologetic when Sammy explained the position. Apparently, quite by chance, he had had an enquiry for that type of engine.

'But why didn't you tell me afore, Sammy? I would have held on to it. Why, it can't be more than ten minutes since the fellow came and took the engine away on his lorry. From up Truro way he was.'

'What kind of lorry was it?' asked Sammy desperately.

'Green, six-wheeler. Name of Bennetts. Can't be far away.'

We leaped into Sammy's car and rushed off along the main road, driving at full speed for several miles, before, abruptly, Sammy stopped.

'It edn't no good; we might spend days trying to find the fellow, and then he might turn awkward.' He sat back, and looked at m 'Oh, dear, oh dear; now what happens? What's my line with Mr Smith?'

Mr Smith, it transpired, was not at all amused. In the course of some acrimonious telephone conversations and a couple of blistering letters, he made it clear he wanted his car back or else …

So one fine day found Sammy trailing miserably up the hill to see Mr Primrose, the solicitor, and explain the sad and sorry story. That elderly, white-haired expert on legal affairs took a caustic view.

'You garage people are all the same, always doing a deal on the spot, thinking you're being smart. When will you learn always to get things down in black and white?'

By now, Sammy was heartily wishing that he had got something down, in black, white or scarlet, for the fact had been triumphantly pointed out, by the solicitor now acting for Mr Smith, that Sammy was not even in possession of the log book of the car, and, therefore, had even less right to sell it to a third party.

For days after this, whenever I saw Sammy, he looked quite worn out with the cares of Mr Smith's car.

'The poor fellow, ee don't know whether ee do be comin' or goin',' remarked Sammy's wife sympathetically one morning, as we watched the harassed man flop into a chair. He shook his head despairingly.

'What do you think he's thought up now? Why, if you like, he's willing to sell me his car for fifty pounds. *Fifty pounds*! Why, the darn thing wasn't worth a penny more'n I gave it for it.'

I must say, I had my doubts over that, but Sammy went on to prove his point by gathering independent quotations from several local garage proprietors as to the approximate value of a car which had been under the sea for several hours. They were all much nearer Sammy's figure than Mr Smith's.

It was no good. A few days later Sammy returned from yet another abortive conference with Mr Primrose.

'Mr Primrose, ee do be all for doin' the right thing, an' the law says this and that, but ee don't get very far on my behalf. Reckon if they go to court you don't stand much chance, ee says. Fat lot o' 'elp that is,' said Sammy, pulling a rude face at the absent Mr Primrose.

But as it happened, with his passion for using legally correct means, Mr Primrose was able to turn up trumps in the eleventh hour, so to speak. A day or two later I came upon Sammy, not working in the garage, but hunched up in his office over a sheaf of accounts.

"Ullo, my fancy,' he said, welcoming me with almost the first smile I could remember ever since the sorry affair began. 'Come and join in the fun and games.'

What Sammy was working upon, it transpired, was Mr Primrose's legal counter-knockout. While, in his opinion, Sammy could not avoid Mr Smith's reasonable demand for £50 or the car, there was, equally, no legal reason why Sammy should not present Mr Smith with a bill for his work in salvaging the grey car from its watery grave.

'And remember,' said Mr Primrose, pursing his lips meaningly, 'make it a *full* and *detailed* statement. Don't overlook *any* cost, however small.'

The penny had dropped with a clang, and Sammy had gone to work with, as you might say, a song in his heart. Now, as I looked over his shoulder, I watched him writing down the fascinating facts and figures:

	£	s.	d.
'To twelve men's wages, at 7/- per hour, approximately four hours hauling car from harbour	16	16	6
'To cost of special hydraulic winches for hauling car out of harbour	6	17	6
'To cost of patent seaweed-removing materials used for cleaning car	4	13	7

And so on, and so forth. Looking through the completed list which Sammy presented for my approval before rushing it up to Mr Primrose, I could not see that there was any item which was technically impossible, even down to the cost of providing refreshments for workers, 30/- ... After all, as Sammy said, men get thirsty, don't they?

When the bill was completed and sent off to Mr Primrose, it came to a grand total of £52 6s. 8d.

'Why the odd £2 6s. 8d.?' I asked.

Sammy winked.

'I might as well make a profit, mightn't I ?'

Well, Sammy certainly never made that profit, but at least he never heard any more from Mr Smith. Soon he began to whistle and sing again, more like the old Sammy. In fact, he is the old Sammy, except for one important respect.

I shouldn't advise anyone to reverse their car into our little harbour here, and then appeal to Sammy Richards for help.

I can just imagine what Sammy would say:

'Sorry ... I just edn't interested.'

VII
Escape

The prisoner knew that his task would take a long time but he had plenty of that: he was prepared to spend weeks, even months in achieving his ultimate goal. Always he waited until evening when he was unlikely to be disturbed, and then he concentrated all his energies on the same small corner of his cell, where there stood a long oblong slab of concrete, a sort of paving stone. With infinite care and patience he would remove the surrounding impediments until the great slab was fully exposed. Then, bending very low so that he could exert the maximum of pressure he would manoeuvre about until at last he managed to take the weight with his fingers and wriggled the slab up out of its socket.

The work was easier after that. The earth underneath was soft and he was able to scoop it out in great handfuls. At first he worked straight downwards, until his hands could reach no further. Then he burrowed sideways, under the adjoining slabs, tearing away the dank soily foundation until he was able to work a slab loose and lift it out. In this way he gradually widened the area of working until the hole he had created was big enough for him to stand in. Then, crouching low, he began to scrape away the earth under his feet, sinking himself lower and lower.

His task was rendered more complicated by the necessity for hiding all traces during daylight hours. He disposed of the surplus earth in several ways. He pressed some of it into the cracks between other floor stones and into the cracks between the walls. He pushed small handfuls into a corner, under the bed, where they were unlikely to be noticed even if the bed was moved. Each day, too, he sprinkled small soil into his lavatory pail, shaking it up until it merged with the other contents. The remaining earth he put back into the hole, using it as material for strengthening the side walls of the hole. The stone slabs he carefully replaced after each night's work, holding them together with wet earth so that they had an effective appearance of solid normality.

For three weeks he lived in a state of painful tension, working himself to exhaustion every night, yet unable to sleep for more than an hour or so during the day for the fear of some unexpected discovery. Each time the warders came round with meals, handing them through the grill, he was careful to place himself in such a position that his body hid the disturbed patch of floor, in case there were signs of his handiwork visible to searching eyes. When the regular cell inspection was made he stood to attention very correctly with his booted feet, fortunately rather large, placed squarely over the stone slabs which hid his fantastic hopes. Yet ... there was just the chance that they were no such fantastic hopes (otherwise he would never have had the energy nor willpower to continue his weary burrowing). Three weeks ago, idly scraping green slime off a corner part of the wall he had wonderingly traced out the unmistakable pattern of a map, scratched deep into the stonework – presumably in the forlorn hope that some day it might prove of help to another inmate of the cell. With the aid of a few blurred words carved under the drawing he was able to understand that there was an underground tunnel running about twenty feet below his cell. Following with a trembling finger the scratched directions on the map he had seen that the tunnel ran away under the prison buildings and far out towards the wild marshlands beyond – to freedom.

It was on the twenty-third night, soon after resuming his regular scraping, that his hands felt the earth loosen and crumble, suddenly disintegrating into surprised space. Crouching down he thrust his arm deep into the blackness, only to feel emptiness. Possessed by a wild surge of joy he began kicking and jumping at the earth underneath him, bringing his whole weight down savagely. At last his feet plunged through the battered soil and he dropped three or four feet on to damp, muddy ground. He crouched there for several minutes, gulping uncomfortably in the strange heavy atmosphere. Everywhere his eyes saw only blackness, a thick swirling blackness that washed over him like the sea. But as he felt cautiously around him his groping hands gradually outlined the circular shape of a tunnel, lined with wet sticky mud. It seemed about four feet wide and rather less in height. He could almost stretch his arms out on both sides, but he had to bend down on to his knees to avoid scraping his head against the roof. There was dampness everywhere; he could feel slow drops of water oozing out of the wet roof and dripping on to his back. The dank air caught at his lungs, starting him coughing and choking.

He climbed back into his cell. He had no knowledge of the exact time, but he estimated that there must be at least three hours before dawn. He hesitated, wondering whether to be cautious and wait for the next night. Into his mind's eyes there surged visions of all the frustrating possibilities of discovery, during the ensuing day. He decided to take the risk then and there. He moved about swiftly in the darkness – tidying up the cell, modelling his pillow into the shape of a sleeping figure under the bed blankets, crawling on his knees over the cold stone slabs and sweeping up the scattered soil. Finally, he crept back into the hole, lowering the heavy stones back into place after him, and jumped down into the tunnel.

Remembering the directions of the map, he took the left turn. He began crawling forward on his hands and knees, sliding each knee forward slowly and uncomfortably, dragging his bent body afterwards. He could feel the wet mud pressing into the thin fabric of his prison costume, clinging to the flesh beneath. Sometimes he inadvertently raised himself and brushed the rough crop of his head against the tunnel roof, and muddy wetness trickled down the side of his face and down his neck. All the time he breathed heavily, the damp air clutching at his throat, weighing on his lungs.

It was impossible to follow the direction of the tunnel, to guess whether it lay straight or whether it twisted and curved. On the map it had seemed a straight line; now, for all he knew, it might be moving round in an endless circle. Dragging himself along laboriously and painfully he could only fix his mind on the single desperate knowledge that somewhere, somehow, the tunnel led to freedom. In the darkness the world seemed to have stopped; or rather, he seemed to have entered some other world, a world weary under the earth's weight. He felt as if he had moved out of the enclosure of his cell walls into equally imprisoning walls of blackness. He began wondering whether other human beings had groped their way through the tunnel – and when and why, and what had happened to them. He supposed that the man who had inscribed the life-saving map on the wall had come that way. Running a dry tongue-tip over slightly swollen lips, the prisoner thought of the other man, also lost in the darkness, also crawling on into the unknown … He tried to visualise the other reaching the end of his journey … the sudden glimpse of light, the wild moment of joy as he emerged into freedom. But the vision eluded him, drowned in blackness.

He thought of his cell, wondering desperately how much evidence he had left there. If only he had had a light of some sort, a torch or even a box of matches – a light would have simplified everything. He projected his thoughts ahead to the time of the warder's arrival with breakfast in the morning. He visualised the rap on the door, the unusual suggestive silence, the querying face at the grill … the look of surprise turning to anger … the rattle of keys, the crunch of boots on the floor. The warder would have a torch (it would still be dusky in the cell). He saw the beam of the torch sweeping round the room, bathing everything in a merciless spotlight. The tidy bed, with its lifeless, artificial figure; the suspiciously neat appearance of the cell itself; the floor – would there be a faint tell-tale line of disturbed soil, a faint incriminating crevice between the stones, an uneven angle to the stones? He saw the warder move swiftly forwards, saw the short squat figure bending down – excited realisation illuminating his dull features. He heard the warder's sharp exclamation, his shrill call to other warders; heard, from afar, the gathering rumble of boots echoing across the stones. The warders would gather in a circle over the bland stone faces, pulling and tugging and heaving … far away, any moment, a draught of threatening air might plunge into the blackness of the tunnel.

He shivered at his thoughts. The air around him was cold and damp, laden with tremendous hidden weights. Suddenly he felt frightened to think of the fantastic tonnage of suffocating soil, rising above him to some distant night sky. The realisation that he was underground, burrowing like some prehistoric animal, struck him sharply, sending a faint nerve throbbing in his head. He became filled with an urgent desire to push back the blackness that was creeping over him, to hurry forwards towards some miraculous outlet. But he found it impossible to hasten ... he could only go on with long, slow movements. Each contact with the moist earth seemed more repugnant. Sometimes a wave of nausea swept over him as his groping hands plunged into sticky heaps of mud. Once his fingers closed on the soft jelly-like shape of something alive – a worm or a small snake – and he screamed with the horror of it. His voice rose up sharply then died away strangely, deadened by the clinging dampness. He tried to wipe away the offensive feeling ... but each time he clutched wet mud after that it seemed for a moment that he was clutching a fat snake, and he had to struggle not to scream again.

Now and then he stopped and measured the shape and width of the tunnel. He was filled with a recurring fear that, in some subtle menacing way, the tunnel was narrowing and closing on him. He found some temporary re-assurance in stretching out his arms and proving that there was no change in width. He wished he could have measured the direction of the tunnel with the same ease, that he could have traced its steady climb towards a starlit night sky. Then he could have banished an itching worry that the tunnel might, instead, be burrowing downwards – down and down and down into the bowels of the earth. He raised his head and peered worriedly through the blackness, hoping to see some miraculous sign of life – the faint wink of a star, the glimmering moonlight of another world.

He became aware of a growing weariness, guessed that he had been crawling for several hours – perhaps four or five. Each effort was becoming more difficult, each rest more frequent and necessary. Once more he stopped, lying forward on his stomach to ease the steady aching of his leg and thigh muscles, slightly relieving a pain across his back. He felt into his pocket for the stale crust of bread he had brought and began munching it eagerly. Soon his hunger became governed by the knowledge that it was all the food he had, and he began taking very small bites, chewing them with careful slowness. The feel of the coarse grains passing down his throat warmed him and gave him a flash of new strength. When he had eaten half of it he put it back in his pocket, becoming aware as he did so of a sudden thirst. He scooped a hand into the muddy water that lined his pathway, raising it to his mouth. Wincing at the thick slimy taste he managed to swallow a few drops of mud-flavoured liquid. He coughed once or twice, spitting out pieces of dirt. Then he lay forward again, letting his body sink luxuriously into the soft mud. He lay there drowsily, listening in fascination to the faint music of water dripping from the tunnel roof, splashing on to the muddy ground. He felt his body crying out sensually for him to let the beautiful finality of sleep sweep up over him, out of the blackness. His head sank lower and lower, his eyes closing. Then he felt the thick mud oozing into his nostrils, clinging to his lips, and he started up into terrified awakeness.

Spitting out the taste of mud, he began crawling forward again. Now, in order to control his mind, he started counting his movements. One-two, one-two, one-two, one-two, for each movement of a knee. He found that the rhythm of counting helped him to maintain a more regular passage. Then the weight of the effort began to drag on his body like the burden of increasingly heavier chains. Slowly, against his will, he found the movements slackening, the counting faltering. His thoughts began to wander again, struggling to formulate odd ideas. Supposing he was lost? Supposing he had taken the wrong turning? Supposing the map had been a hoax? (But no, it had been accurate enough about the tunnel being underneath his cell.) All the same, supposing? ... Once he even glanced over his shoulder, prepared in a vivid moment of emotion to see a distant artificial glimmer, to hear the dread slouching movements of ghostly searching warders. If he listened he could imagine hearing the sounds of crawling men – or was it only the dripping of water? The warders would be well equipped – torches and rifles. He shuddered: almost seeing the stab of bright light, almost hearing the staccato sound of the shot, almost feeling the searing thrust of pain.

His movements gradually became reduced to their slowest; great painful gropings forward. It seemed that as he got more tired so the air became heavier and more difficult to breathe. But somehow he kept on, squelching through the mud like a lumbering snail. He had to fight continually against the threatening desire for sleep, had to mutter and mumble to himself to keep alive some semblance of consciousness. Now he no longer seemed to be moving of his own efforts, but to be floating through the darkness on the soft moving back of the mud. At some isolated moment he ate the remainder of the bread, choked down more muddy water. He had lost all count of time, only sensing, dimly, that whole hours – perhaps the whole night, perhaps another day – must have passed. Burrowing on his eternal endless journey, he began to feel there were whole years, escaped into timelessness, since he climbed out of the dry four walls of his cell.

It did not seem real to him when at last the change began. He had begun to give himself up to the embrace of the darkness, to loose himself into the mystic void of perpetual night. Looking forward – through mud-flecked, half-closed eyes – he was hardly conscious at first of the faint weakening in the colour of the darkness, hardly aware that the clouds were less full of drowning blackness. Not until he had crawled forward with many more painful movements did he assimilate the full meaning of the gathering grey tint, of the faint shimmering fringe of whiteness ... Then he saw the far away pinpoint of light. It leapt into his life, dancing towards him along a shaft of greyness, piercing through the angry waves of darkness. He wanted to lie down and swoon with sudden released happiness; delirious strength surged into his weary body and he wanted to shout out for joy, but found the words crackled weirdly in his dry mouth. Mumbling a frantic prayer, he began crawling forward, pressing his knees with savage triumph through the clinging mud and clutching with feverish excitement at the slimy walls.

Now, at last, he felt the tunnel climbing and rising. he crawled swiftly along the greyish path, drawing nearer and nearer to the light. The pinpoint grew larger and through it, suddenly, he saw the startling gold of a new day, the azure blue of to-morrow's sky, speckled with filmy clouds. Filled with insane happiness he stumbled up the last slope and out of the tunnel.

He found himself standing in a small quarry pit. A few quick footsteps took him over the brink, into a world of dazzling sunshine and rambling grey commonland. For a moment he paused, closing his eyes and drinking in great gulps of fresh, free air.

Then, abruptly, he became aware of the great bareness of the fields around him, of the long shadow he cast as the sun spotlighted his small speck for all the world to see. Suppressing an uneasy desire to look back over his shoulder he clenched his fingers tight into the palms of his hands, and went forward.

He walked out into the unknown summer morning. And as he walked the long rows of bushy-faced hedges bristled treacherously in the breeze, alive and unfriendly; the occasional solitary trees lurked menacingly in their own shadows. Ahead of him, as far as his tired eyes could see, the very horizon rose up into the sky. It surrounded him, grey and towering, like an endless wall – and as insurmountable. Soon he would begin to feel himself being watched, a peeping warder behind each puffy cloud ...

VIII

The Man from the Ministry

The first time I met the Man from the Ministry (I wish it had been the last) was one evening during the last winter of the second war, at that semi-dusky period when one had a hazy guilty notion that the blackout was about due. I was trying resolutely to stir myself from the depths of a resilient armchair in order to carry out the irritating but necessary ceremony, when there came a peremptory rat-tat-tat-tat-TAT on the door of my flat. Opening it I found myself face to face with a neat, rabbit-faced little man wearing a gleaming new ARP uniform and over-big air-raid warden's helmet – tilted so far back on his head that it pushed his ears out like two grotesque flaps, thus emphasising the resemblance to a rabbit. I was at least one foot taller than the little man but, instinctively, I felt at an uneasy disadvantage.

He did not waste time but, fixing on me a couple of gimlet-like eyes that conveyed quite unmistakably an attitude of strong disapproval, snapped out:

'Do you realise, sir, that it is now two-thirds of a minute past black-out time and your light is still blazing away?'

He paused, not to allow me to answer but merely to take breath, then went on:

'It's a good thing everyone isn't as careless as you, young man, or else I don't know what would happen. We can't run a war half-heartedly, young man. We must have discipline, co-ordination – *efficiency*! The law states explicitly that the blackout should be done at a precise time – a time stated quite clearly in your daily newspaper and on the wireless. You have no excuse, sir, no excuse whatever. However, as this is the first warning, we will make an exception and take no further proceedings. But I warn you, young man, as an authorised official of the appropriate Government Department I cannot allow non-conformity with rules and regulations.'

With which he emitted a small but expressive snort, tossed a final withering glance of scorn in my direction, turned smartly and marched away. I heard his feet going down the stairs, one-two, one-two, in neat and ordered rhythm.

I must admit that even this first encounter preyed on my mind for quite a while, especially while I thought out all the crushing rejoinders and witty sallies I ought to have made. But then the war ended, and in the whirl of excited events of that period I assumed that the Man from the Ministry would have disappeared forever.

I was wrong. I met him again, and again.

The first occasion was when I was completing negotiations for a peacetime job, one ideally suited to my qualifications. At the last moment an urgent letter summoned me to the Ministry. On arrival I filled up an entrance form, also a form stating my business. I took my place in a queue. At last I passed up some stairs and joined another queue. Abruptly I was ushered into a small office. There was the little man sitting at a desk opposite.

He did not seem to remember me in particular, though he cast me an immediate look of distrust and suspicion. Beside him he had files, letters, clippings. He prodded an expert finger among these, drew out a bundle of correspondence tied with a red ribbon. He flipped through the letters irritably.

'This won't do. This won't do at all, young man. Attempting to secure employment on your initiative – ignoring the officially recognised channels established by the Ministry. Dear me, this is most disturbing. Are you aware that you have committed several criminal offences? Not to mention the fact that you have not filled up forms CM/1256 and ABC/234. Neither, it seems, have you complied with the regulations contained in paras 3, 4, 6, 8 and 12, Section Four, Employment Order 51.'

He fixed a sharp look on me.

'Well? What have you to say?'

I felt my lips trembling. Nervously, I ran a hand round the edge of my collar.

'I'm very sorry. I had no idea. I only thought –'

'Quite. Well, we'll give you the benefit in this instance. The best thing you can do is to obtain a copy of the Ministry's booklet on Authorised Employment. That sets out the various procedures necessary to make an application. Then ask the girl at the front desk for the appropriate forms.'

'Yes,' I said. 'I'll do that. But I was wondering, about my proposed job –?'

The small eyes gleamed dangerously.

'Young man, you are being very awkward. The Government has the whole matter in hand. It is essential to proceed only through authorised channels. You have already upset our routine. Now please go. You will hear from us in due course.'

The next time we met was rather unexpectedly. It was some months later. I was still waiting for my employment to be officially arranged. In the meantime, to keep myself occupied, I was trying to clear up the weeds and debris in our back-garden. It is true that, throwing some withered foliage over the wall, I apparently hit the little man on the head as he was passing – but then I imagine he was about to peep over in any case.

'Aha,' he said. His face positively lit up. 'May I inquire precisely what is being done here to this garden?'

I looked round puzzledly at the clumps of unkempt grass, the pit-hole made by an incendiary bomb, the overgrown flower beds.

'I was going to clear up, make a vegetable plot.'

'Indeed? May I see your Ministry authorisation?'

'I didn't know –'

'My dear young man, only under the most *exceptional* circumstances can the Ministry allow unco-ordinated agricultural development by a private individual. Have you a green priority docket?'

'Why, er – no.'

'Tut – tut. Are you a recognised agricultural labourer?'

'No, but –'

'It is all very improper. I will have to arrange for a Ministry Inspector to come and make a report. He may recommend a prosecution. The Ministry feels most strongly about this sort of unauthorized action.'

Unexpectedly, the tight little face curved into a smile. A sardonic smile.

'And what, may I ask, were you proposing to grow?'

'Greens and things. Potatoes –'

'*Potatoes*! Without consulting the list of Specified Standardised Sizes?'

'Well –'

'What else? Carrots, by any chance?'

'Why, yes, carrots – and cabbage and –'

'There is a separate Ministry Order appertaining to carrots, which I cannot possibly outline to you now in detail. But I must tell you young man, that you have behaved most rashly. I only hope you are able to give the inspector some sort of satisfactory explanation.'

Well, after that, it seemed that I was always meeting the Man from the Ministry. There was the time when I wanted to send a Christmas present of a book to my aunt in South Africa. He was there, tense and wary, behind the wire counter – oh, he wasn't fooled for a moment. Had I read the Post Office Regulations? Had I filled in the appropriate details on the appropriate form? Was I a relative of my aunt? – what he meant was had I any *proof*? We spent the morning poring over thick wads of Post Office Statutory procedures and regulations. There seemed some obscure point about the method of sending parcels to South Africa, and this the little man could not clear up. He sent me home, still clutching the parcel. I was to receive an official communication in due course.

Later, there were rather impatient encounters over petrol coupons, clothing coupons, travelling to the Channel Isles, changing a ration book, obtaining fuel, and, of course, income tax. Then came the horrible climax.

It was some years after the war. I was still hoping to be able to build a house, even a small hut, for myself and my family. There were holes in the ceilings and cracks in the walls of our old home. I had been unable to find the right forms to fill up to obtain necessary repairs. At last, in desperation, goaded on by the pitiful cries of my shivering children and the quiet suffering I read in my wife's eyes, I approached a local builder whose yard was stacked with bricks. Furtively I bought from him a quantity of bricks and mortar and arranged for them to be delivered to a plot of wild moorland just outside our village. I had decided to build my own house.

All that first day I sweated and toiled, levelling out the

ground, marking trenches and other measurements. And all the time I worked I felt nervous tingles at my spine – was continually peeping up and down the lane in dread of seeing a familiar figure approaching.

When I reached home late in the evening I was tired beyond belief. I threw myself into an armchair, put my feet on the mantelpiece, and stared into the fire, dozing and half-listening to the wireless. There was some sort of a talk going on …

Suddenly everything burred and crackled. For a moment there was dead silence. Then a strange, metallic voice broke across the ether. It said:

'Calling Car 123. Calling Car 123. Special order from Headquarters. Go to Forty-Four Berry Avenue, pick up owner of house. Young man about thirty-five, dark greasy hair, pale ugly face, shifty eyes, twitching lower lip. Said person suspected of offences against the Housing, Erection by Private Individuals, Act, also of offences against Politeness to Post Office Servants Act. Strongly believed to be further responsible for wide number of offences against various Ministry Orders. May be dangerous. Take full precautions. That is all.'

Immediately the full implications of the message registered on my mind I jerked into frantic action. I made a bee-line for the front door, tugged it open. Then I froze into immobility: there on the door-step was the Man from the Ministry. He was as small and rabbity as ever, but he now wore the austere uniform of a police constable.

He came in, and I fell back nervously before him.

'So you thought you would escape justice, did you?' he said. 'Very foolish of you, young man, very foolish. You should know by now that when an authorised officer of the appropriate Government Department gets an order that order is carried out. No matter what the consequences!' He glared very sternly at me.

'No matter *what* the consequences,' he repeated, as if to squash any ideas I might have about attempting to make a fight for it.

'You've – you've no right to come intruding like this!' I blustered, making an attempt to gather dignity about me.

'Oh, no?' chuckled the intruder. He opened his rather pointed mouth and exposed a flashing row of gold-plated teeth. But in a moment the smile had faded. Instead the teeth became bared, the lips were drawn back, and I nearly cried out, thinking I was looking at a tiger.

'You've committed a grave offence against the Government. You must come along with me, young man,' he hissed, and gripped one of my arms as if his hand was a steel clamp. The next thing I knew he had whirled me round once or twice in mid-air and thrown me over his shoulder like a sack of potatoes.

As soon as we were outside in the street I was struck with the terrifying thought that all my neighbours would witness my humiliation; me a big hulking fellow, letting myself be carried off by this little numbskull. But try as I might I could not move an inch out of his grasp.

I resorted to flattery.

'Please, sir!' I said. 'I'll be good if you let me walk beside you.'

But he took no notice at all, and we went on marching steadily down the garden path. As we did so I heard an endless opening of doors. I wasn't able to see anyone, perhaps fortunately, but I heard them calling out, and my blood curdled … 'Traitor!' 'Black Marketeer!' 'Quisling!' 'Hang him!' 'Shooting's too good for him!' … And after each shout a door banged derisively, and with an air of finality.

Outside there was a black maria waiting. As we approached the back door opened silently. The little man pitched me head-first into the back, shut the door and got into the driving seat. I was enveloped in darkness, but I heard the sound of other people breathing.

'Excuse me!' I whispered, 'where are they taking us? What's happening? Why are we being taken away?'

There were three or four guttural laughs.

'Why do you think? The Ministry has been too clever for us!' said someone in a tone of resignation. Then, after a pause, 'Such a pity. I had a marvellous scheme all worked out for breeding my own hens without a Ministry of Agriculture priority permit.'

'Ah, yes,' said another voice, 'and I – I had nearly completed a most elaborate plan for spending a week by the seaside outside the Government's Holiday Ration Period.'

'Why, you're bad citizens,' I cried out angrily.

They laughed. '*We* are bad citizens! That's a good one. What about you? It's no use pretending now. We know you are the greatest bad citizen of all but – well, this time, the Ministry has been too clever. We must give them their due.'

'Yes, yes,' said the others.

Eventually the car came to a stop and we were taken out one by one, blindfolded, and led into what was obviously a police station. There we had to stand in a row while the tiny cracked voice of our captor read out thirty-three different charges.

'For all of these men I demand the death sentence!' he cried at the end.

There was an ominous pause. I managed to peep out of the corner of my handkerchief. To my horror I saw, sitting high up on a judge's bench, the unmistakable figure of the Man from the Ministry, his sharp little features poking out from under a white woolly wig. He began pronouncing death sentences, gabbling them out in a row.

'It's a frame-up! A frame-up! I want a proper trial!' I cried out, but somehow the words seemed to float away and become distorted so that no one seemed to hear them. Meanwhile after each pronouncement I heard a sharp plop and the sound of a body falling. At last after the thirty-second sentence there was a draught beside me and a hard thud.

I felt a chill at my heart. But there was an evident pause in the proceedings. Perhaps, I thought, in relief, they've only been having me on.

'Your Honour,' I said humbly. 'I'm sure you realise now that this is all a dreadful mistake. However, I'm willing to say no more about it if –'

'Silence!' said the stern, terrible voice. I peeped out of the corner of my bandage and was horrified to see the Judge's face swollen to an enormous size, and going red and purple with anger. Suddenly he bent forward and stuck out a long yellow tongue, like a snake, in my direction.

'You!' he hissed, 'will not be shot – you will be buried alive in a file of official forms!'

'No!' I shouted. 'No!'

I tried to struggle, but a hundred pairs of hands seemed to fasten around me and began dragging me away. They carried

me off into some underground prison and threw me into a
dark cell. I lay there shaking with terror.

After a time I revived and began banging and shouting. A
warder came and peeped through.

'I demand to see the Governor!' I shouted desperately.

The warder laughed.

'All right,' he said, surprisingly. 'Come along.'

He took my arm and we walked through a maze of
corridors. Every now and then we tripped over crumpled
objects.

'Evaders of Ministerial Directives,' said the warder. '*Dead*
ones.' I began shivering.

At last we went through an iron-barred door and into a
room with a long highly polished floor. As soon as I trod on
the floor I slipped over and sat down. I heard the cackling of
laughter, and looked round in wonderment, since the warder
had already disappeared. Then I saw a huge desk at the far end
of the room, behind it a dim figure.

'Oh, sir! – your Honour, your Grace,' I said. Then my feet
shot away and I fell down again.

Cackle, cackle, cackle from the desk.

I made several more attempts. Eventually I was reduced to
crawling along on my stomach. In this manner I reached the
edge of the desk and managed to drag myself up.

'Your Honour, I'm sure, as Governor of this prison, you will
appreciate that there must have been a mistake. I'm a
respectable citizen, I've never done anything wrong at all. I can
get my friends to vouch for me – I've always paid my income
tax …'

I stopped thunderstruck, as I found myself staring into the
mocking eyes of Prison Governor, the Man from the Ministry.

'Well, well, well!' he said. 'So you don't like the conditions
at this prison?' His face became stern. 'Very well, I'll have you
disposed of at once!'

'Oh, no!' I pleaded. 'No, really, I've no complaint!'

'It's too late,' he snapped. He pressed a bell, and four
enormous uniformed warders came in. They all bore a striking
resemblance to him.

'My sons,' he explained. 'We like to keep things in the
family. 'Bring in the file!' snapped the Governor.

They trundled in a huge file, the size of a trunk.

'You can't do this!' I yelled, wild with despair. 'I'm a British citizen, I've constitutional rights ... I – I demand to be allowed to see the Home Secretary.'

The four warders paused. The little man gazed at me from under lowered brows.

'The Home Secretary? He's in Scotland.'

'Well I still want to see him,' I stammered.

'Oh, very well, very well. What a lot of bother!' He pressed another button, took up a telephone receiver, dialled a number.

'Hullo, is that Glasgow? Is that you, Sec.? There's a chap here wants to see you. Yes, I know, it's a nuisance. Better hop down, though. I want to get the case over – it's my week-end off.'

'He'll be here in a minute,' he said.

We sat around waiting, the four warders with folded arms. Eventually there was a whining noise. 'I'll go and let him in," said the Governor.

He walked over to the door and opened it. Outside I saw the majestic figure of the Home Secretary, wearing black flowing robes. The two of them came walking towards me.

I went down on my knees, my hands up in an attitude of prayer.

'Oh, Home Secretary, please investigate my case! I'm innocent, I swear I'm innocent.'

'That's what they all say,' prompted the Governor.

'That's what they all say,' said the Home Secretary.

Startled, I looked up and saw that the Home Secretary's face was absolutely blank, bereft of features.

'I reject your appeal,' murmured the Governor.

'I reject your appeal,' mumbled the blank face of the Home Secretary.

The Man from the Ministry winked at me.

'He's a dummy, see? Makes it much simpler.' He smiled proudly. For the first time I noticed his hand was behind the Secretary.

'See, I can make him nod and speak just by pressing a button.'

'But he's got no face,' I cried.

He frowned.

'So he hasn't. I must remedy that.' He made several swift slashes with a fountain pen. 'There, that's better.'

The Home Secretary was now the twin-brother of the Governor, the Judge, the Man from the Ministry.

Suddenly one of the warders called out.

'Boss! We've got the forms all ready.'

'Oh, goodie! Shove him in, boys.'

I struggled frantically.

'No!' I cried out. 'You can't do this. I'm a married man, I've a wife and child. I'm a loyal patriot, I contribute to National Savings. I'm not a criminal!'

'Tut! Tut!' said the Governor. 'We've been over all that.'

He nodded significantly to the men. They picked me up like a child.

'Stop! I'm the wrong man!' I screamed.

'Nonsense!' said the Governor. 'Government Departments never make mistakes. We have your records. Unimpeachable evidence. You have never filled up a single form accurately. Can't have that sort of thing.'

The four men heaved me into mid air. I screamed as I was tossed above the open file. I saw the men gathering great armfuls of paper forms to throw after me. I felt myself falling.

In the last second I caught a glimpse of the Man from the Ministry. He was sitting back, looking highly satisfied, while a pretty blonde waitress began laying a dinner table before him.

'That'll teach the public a lesson, boys!' he was saying, pinching the waitress' thigh and smirking. 'I think we'll put the body on public exhibition as a warning. I'll contact the Ministry of Exhibitions at once.'

The light darkened, and a stream of dry pieces of paper fell upon me, flutering over my face, covering my eyes, my mouth, weighing down upon me with their vast numbers. I could not see, I could not breathe, I was suffocating ...

*

When I awoke I found my wife shaking me urgently by the shoulder, at the same time brushing dust and debris off my face, and from around my neck and shoulders. Another part of the ceiling had collapsed, nearly smothering me.

When at last I had taken a few grateful breaths and recovered from the shock of my dreams I became conscious of an insistent tapping at the door.

'Oh, dear,' said my wife. 'That'll be the gentleman who's just called. He wants to know –'

I staggered to my feet and went to the door.

'Really,' said the Man from the Ministry. 'My time is valuable, I cannot afford to waste it standing on doorsteps.' He cleared his throat officiously.

'I have called here on behalf of the Ministry for the Co-Ordination and Unification of Internal Affairs, Smallholding and General Housing Department. I understand you have applied for permission to build a house. I must warn you it is very unlikely that you can be granted a permit. In the first instance, you are requested to render a statutory declaration of –'

But at that moment all the wrath of ancient ancestors welled up in me. Uttering a wild cry, I leapt at the podgy, inviting throat of the Man from the Ministry. Without stopping to argue he gave a remarkably faithful imitation of a rabbit and within two seconds had reached the end of the garden and vaulted over the gate. My last sight was of his crabbed black-frocked figure scuttling down the street and disappearing into the dusk.

I went back to my fire with an airy, brisk step. I felt I was a man again. And I knew I would remain one henceforth, no matter how many hundreds of their miserable forms I might fill up.

IX

Highest Bid

Mr Watson was a tough, balding and somewhat disillusioned auctioneer who was more than used to the odd ways of mankind and in particular womankind. He had large and rather luxurious offices not far off the West End where he was used to greeting a variety of callers.

From somewhat bitter experience Mr Watson had become used to most of these callers being what in the trade were known as time-wasters – after all, your really fly businessman with a deal to do wasted no time, indeed probably did all the necessary talking in a single phone call.

Unfortunately, for Mr Watson's point of view, there was another kind of caller who not only never dreamed of using the telephone, but equally never imagined calling in just for a minute or a few minutes, but would – if allowed to – happily stay the best part of an afternoon occupying his valuable time.

Consequently, when the little old lady called Miss Palmer was ushered into his office one day clutching tightly her obviously precious parcel Mr Watson, sighing, knew from past experience that he would just have to be patient for a while – at least until she came round to the real point of her visit.

'… quite a family heirloom in its way,' she confessed when at long last she began undoing her parcel, taking off each layer of paper as if unrobing something quite priceless … In the event finally revealing a fair to middling example of an old fashioned Toby jug. 'Yes, this is it. Once upon a time, a *long time ago* of course, you understand, this used to belong to my mother.'

As she spoke, Miss Palmer almost winced at the use of the past tense, and it seemed as if her eyes went a little moist. Mr Watson could only look away uncomfortably.

'Well, er,' he began.

'Of course,' said Miss Palmer, half to herself, obviously already forgetting about her audience. 'Of course I suppose I'm really being just a sentimental old thing. But you see – well, I can't help remembering how my dear mother used to tell how my grandmother always kept the jug on the mantelpiece – yes, indeed, this didn't just belong to my mother, it was in the family for a long, long time – yes, and my grandmother treasured it from her mother – and then in turn, my own mother, well she looked after it so carefully and when, before – well, anyway, as I think I was telling you, it ended up as a kind of family heirloom.'

'And I suppose,' said Mr. Watson patiently, 'I suppose you've got rather attached to it yourself, now? I mean, with all those past associations, you must be very fond –'

'Yes, yes, of course.'

Miss Palmer smiled, a faded, rather sad smile.

'Yes, but ...' Her voice was suddenly rather quiet. 'Well, the fact is, in my present circumstances ...'

Mr Watson coughed, and stood up. He had been through many such interviews, encountered many such moments – and knew it was best to stand up decisively, else he would be here trapped for the rest of the working afternoon.

'Quite, quite.' He hummed and hawed a little, and made some sort of pretence at looking at the Toby jug. 'Mmmmmh, yes, a nice little piece.'

He looked sharply at Miss Palmer, but she showed no reaction. He doubted if she had the remotest idea how much the Toby jug was worth – or rather, he thought ironically, not worth.

'Well, anyway,' he said, with a subtle indication of dismissal. 'Don't you worry ma'am. Just you leave this with me, and I'll do my very best on your behalf, I promise.'

Miss Palmer looked a trifle uncertain, but eventually she went out, with one last lingering look at the Toby jug. Mr Watson watched her go with some misgivings: it was, after all, several days to the auction.

As he expected, the next day Miss Palmer was back in the office again, all tight and taut and full of new determination, saying that she had decided not to part with her precious jug after all.

The following day, of course, sheepishly, she brought it back again. And after that, she kept away, though Mr Watson had some faint idea of the turmoil raging in her quiet and normally placid little heart.

On the day of the auction the hall was crowded to capacity with the usual conglomeration of dealers, buyers, and the merely curious. There were several lots to get through that day, and Mr Watson found himself busy with his hammer and gavel shouting the number, taking the bids up sometimes into the eighties and nineties, for some inlaid walnut furniture.

He was so busy, in fact, that he hardly remembered Miss Palmer, until at last, he came to: 'Lot 145, 1 period Toby jug ...' and he paused and looked around. There she was tucked in a distant corner seeming almost to belong to the furniture and the period pieces.

Mr Watson smiled and nodded, as if to convey again, 'Don't worry ma'am, I'll do my best': and then in a brisk businesslike voice he drew attention to the superlative qualities of this genuine and most original piece of real Staffordshire pottery.

The bidding, as Mr Watson had secretly feared, was not half as brisk as his introduction: Toby jugs were, these days, an uncertain element. However, there was one dealer he had his eye on who specialised in the jugs, and he was hoping to land the sale with him. Slowly the bidding progressed ...

'Fourteen pounds,' said Mr Watson at last, repeating the dealer's latest bid with some satisfaction: it was in his opinion a fair price. 'Fourteen pounds I am bid for this –'

Mr Watson's stentorian voice was cut short by a bid of fourteen pounds and twenty five pence. He frowned, looked puzzledly around, and then inquiringly at the dealer-specialist who, much to Mr Watson's relief nodded.

'Fourteen pounds fifty pence,' said Mr Watson quickly, and then, hurriedly, 'Going – going –'

'Fourteen pounds seventy-five pence.'

Mr Watson glanced and then looked beseechingly at the dealer. By some supreme effort he willed the dealer to bid fifteen pounds. Back came the answering bid; by which time the dealer himself was perhaps a little piqued. But he went on to fifteen pounds seventy-five pence.

But there, Mr Watson could see quite clearly, the dealer was sticking; and it was with real anguish that he heard the firm, clear, rather reed-like voice pipe up from the back of the hall, 'Sixteen, er, pounds …'

At the end of the auction Mr Watson was still muttering to himself about women and sentiment, and old fools who bothered him and all that sort of thing; and moving sheets of paper about trying to get his things cleared up. He was not too busy, however, to observe the frail old lady who sidled, shamefacedly, up to his table.

'Well,' said Mr Watson with heavy sarcasm. 'Well, well –'

He was about to say something more when he took a good look at the face of Miss Palmer, who had just quite crazily bid sixteen pounds for her own Toby jug. It was a finely formed, once pretty face of a sweet old lady, and Mr Watson didn't like to see the rings under the eyes, and the generally pinched look.

'Oh, dear,' said Miss Palmer apologetically. 'I'm afraid that when I thought of my jug going to that dealer and being put in a shop window like – like an orphan, I just couldn't help bidding.'

'Ummmmh,' said Mr Watson sternly. He cleared his throat officiously. 'Well, as it happens I'm afraid your bid was *too late*.'

For a few seconds Mr Watson paused in order to punish Miss Palmer a little with her own dismay, then he went on.

'Your jug was sold for fifteen pounds seventy-five pence. However,' Mr Watson coughed and busied himself with a cheque book. 'As it happens the bidder decided he didn't want the jug after all and he, er, asked me to return it to you, er, with his compliments.'

'But –' began Miss Palmer, tremulously.

Mr Watson smiled blandly.

'But me no buts, dear lady. Or as the saying goes, er – never look a gift horse in the face. Mmmmh.'

'But, Mr Watson, I don't quite understand.'

Miss Palmer stood there indecisively, looking puzzledly from Mr Watson to the Toby jug, and then back to the auctioneer again. Her face was all puckered and creased, as if in some desperate way she was trying to understand something that would always remain a little outside her comprehension.

'Shhhh!' said Mr Watson. 'Not another word, dear lady. There is nothing more to be said.'

In one magnificent movement, Mr Watson, who could be most efficient when he wanted, placed in Miss Palmer's arms a Toby jug – plus a cheque of his own for fifteen pounds seventy-five pence, and began to escort her towards the office door.

Allowing Miss Palmer absolutely no more ifs and buts, etc., he propelled her gently but firmly out into the wide, wide world.

For a time he stood in the doorway and watched the frail and somehow bewildered figure as it gradually disappeared down the busy street; then, shaking his head in amusement over the sentimentality that could render even auctioneers human, Mr Watson returned to business – and began working out to the exact penny the commission due to him from his next client.

X

My Uncle Who Paints Pictures

The very first time I met my Uncle Hamish he opened up an entirely new world for me. I could see Mr Gladstone sunbathing in a top hat and a pair of pink shorts, Queen Elizabeth dancing the Charleston across a wide green lawn, Cleopatra winding her serpent shape around a lamp-post, Vesta Tilley singing to an audience of horses, and a man with a pipe and a bowler hat taking an afternoon nap while a cloud of hornets gathered around him (Mr Baldwin, I later realised). It was all exciting and exotic, and I just stared and stared; though what intrigued me most, in the end, was the blank half of the picture. When I asked Uncle Hamish he looked mysterious and boomed out, epigrammatically: 'Why, that's life, friend! Finished when you think it's only half finished!' But the very way he spoke made me feel sure of some deep hidden meaning or implication behind the evasiveness. At any rate for days and days afterwards I kept thinking and worrying about it all. This fact, alone, inclines me to look upon Uncle Hamish as a painter of potential greatness, even though I did accidentally discover that, in this instance, my uncle just ran out of paints and couldn't be bothered to go out to buy any more.

That's how it is most of the time with my uncle. Never at a loss for a subject for a picture, he seldom has the patience to complete it. This is a great pity. If only he had finished some of his less obscure pictures he might well have succeeded in fulfilling his life-long ambition of having a picture hung in an art gallery. But there, we must grant the artist his temperament, his little caprices. My uncle spending a lifetime starting several hundreds of pictures, other artists spending a lifetime finishing merely one – it's all a matter of choice. In the case of my uncle, too, it has to be remembered that he has other vocations in life. Painting might easily be put aside for several months while my uncle engages in building a summer-house, or learning to fly an aeroplane, or singing opera or, as on one occasion, knitting his own clothes. (I think my uncle had been reading too much William Morris or Eric Gill ... but had you seen him, day after day, sitting out in the garden, knee deep in balls of wool, with long knitting needles continually falling out of his fingers or sticking into his thighs – well, you would, at least, have credited him with very great perseverance.)

However, it is with Uncle Hamish as a painter that I am concerned here, even if, as alas! there are indications, no one else seems much concerned to date. I am a little vague as to how or why my uncle took up painting. He himself, if asked, would probably throw out some witticism about taking it up to pass the time. It appears fairly certain, as one or two visitors have been heard to say, that he never had painting lessons. Unfortunately, there are few records of my uncle's earliest attempts at the art. His sister once confided to me, apparently without any sense of shame, that she used to pick up his old canvases and use them for wrapping up parcels to her cousin out in the Indian Army. As her cousin has since been eaten by a boa-constrictor it appears impossible to take any further steps in the matter. So by such queer tricks of destiny are we robbed of valuable data about our native geniuses.

The first painting by my Uncle Hamish that I have actually been able to trace is a study of an oblong-shaped object tied together with a ribbon. The only clue to its identity is the label BOX on the back. I am inclined to think it is meant to be a chocolate box, having worked out that, at the time it was painted, Uncle Hamish was very fond of chocolates. My uncle, whose memory is rather vague, has put forward the intriguing theory that the shape is that of a coffin. To substantiate this he has recollected that about the period when the picture was painted the decease occurred of his Grandfather Pelly, who used to twist his ears and whom, consequently, he hated. The fact that the ribbon is painted green with red spots is psychologically highly significant in the opinion of my uncle, who, as any student of his paintings will have observed, has made a study, if a rather swift and superficial one, of the works

of Freud and Jung. However that may be, the painting is not
what an exacting critic would call a representative one. In fact,
one has to pass quickly through several stacks of canvases
before reaching what may truthfully be termed the important
ones. The first of these is perhaps the action picture of a
football in mid-air. I don't suppose any painter before – unless
it be some despicable hack producing an advertisement for a
firm of football manufacturers – thought of making a football
the subject of a work of art. Many people might suppose it to
be a somewhat difficult task. My uncle tossed it off in a couple
of hours. Apart from one or two minor details, such as the
irregular shape of the ball and the fact that it is painted
crimson with white spots, I think he has produced a most
original painting. If only you could have half an hour's chat
with my uncle before actually looking at the picture I am
convinced you would share my opinion. The value of the chat
is that some background information, which naturally could
not all be included in the picture, can be sketched in. Thus, you
would be able, more easily, to appreciate that the football is
not just a football but a symbol of humanity. Knowing this you
would be a little nearer to grasping the significance of the
crimson – which, of course, is the blood shed by suffering
humanity. The white represents the good among humanity.
And so on and so on, until everything becomes perfectly clear.

Already, you will observe, my Uncle Hamish was showing
strong Impressionistic leanings. Later these became even more
pronounced, particularly in such pictures as *Smoke*. In this a
real cigar is stuck with glue across the middle of the canvas and
(whenever someone is to inspect the picture) lit up by my uncle.
Perhaps even more representative is the epic *Blast*, for the
purpose of which my uncle spent no less than £20 on the
purchase of a glittering new trumpet. The trumpet is inserted
in one corner of the canvas symbolising the voice, or blast, or
aroused mankind. It is a feature of this, as of many other of my
uncle's pictures – and one which I am inclined to think will
enhance their value some day, from the connoisseur's point of
view – that several patches of canvas remain unpainted (save
for one or two instances, as in the case of *Blast*, where, in an
idle moment, my uncle scribbled in a pencil sketch of a kettle,
probably in practice for some larger portrait).

Those are but two examples of Uncle Hamish's Impressionistic period. If only I had the time I could tell you about even more original works, involving the use of human hair, baked bean cans, piano keys, hand-mirrors, fountain pens, the driving wheel of a car ... and, in a great many cases, railway tickets, bus time-tables and daily newspapers, which my uncle, a forgetful man, was always stuffing into his pockets. Later there came the inevitable Romantic period, which produced a succession of still-life studies, about the execution of which my uncle still speaks with a faintly suggestive twinkle in his eyes. From talks I have had with my uncle I realise that something really remarkable might have been achieved here if he had been given a free hand. It was his idea, for instance, to insert into pictures living eye-brows, real fleshy cheeks and, perhaps, finger-tips and ears, not to mention other portions of the human body. Unfortunately he found the difficulties of arranging for supplies rather beyond him. About these nude studies, then, there is not a great deal I can say, other than to emphasise that they were ambitious in scope, grandiose in execution and exciting to view. Practically every one, however, was destroyed on a bonfire by my uncle's wife.

Perhaps it would be as well to devote a paragraph here to Uncle Hamish's wife. It has to be admitted that without her help my uncle's artistic career might long ago have been brought to an abrupt end. My uncle was never reared with the idea of working for a living. When, at the tender age of thirty-three, he suddenly found himself entirely devoid of means through the concurrent bankruptcy and decease of his parents, he was confronted with the Crisis of his life. How fortunate that just at this period he should meet the young, impressionable and, if rather plain, *rich* Gladiola, daughter of the owner of a vast patent medicine business which was bound to thrive continuously. Very wisely, I feel, my uncle did not so much *show* his pictures to his wife-to-be as *describe* them; and my uncle is a very effective conversationalist. The upshot of it all was that Uncle Hamish and Gladiola were married, with a blaze of publicity and presents, and my uncle's future was settled. His wife, in addition to providing unquestioning adoration, a liberal cash allowance and many other comforts, also bought a large country house in which what was previously a baronet's drinking parlour was converted into a studio for my uncle.

For a long time life proceeded smoothly at my uncle's new home. Each of his new pictures was framed in the very best gilded frame and hung in a position of prominence. In time, the pictures spread further and further throughout the house. Soon there was an average of four to each living-room, one at every twenty yards' interval along the corridors, at least two to every bedroom, three in the bathroom (as my uncle said, people should be glad of *something* to look at during a bath) and one in the little room adjoining (because *there* dilly-dallying was not really to be encouraged). As I say, this displaying of my uncle's pictures went on for a long time, but gradually some sort of subtle change obviously took place. One by one pictures began to disappear, although fortunately this did not seem to bother my Uncle Hamish. From investigations I have made I rather suspect the whole delicate business was engineered by his wife – not, I hasten to say, so much on her own desire (after all she had married my uncle and taken him for better or worse) but because she found it increasingly difficult to keep or even obtain any domestic staff. Cooks would have fainting fits on coming upon a more Impressionistic study in a darkened pantry; housemaids would cry out hysterically as their unsuspecting shoulders brushed against a mop of human hair jutting out from a painted chin; once a chauffeur developed a phobia that he could not drive the car into the garage because one of Uncle Hamish's larger pictures, parked there as there was no room anywhere else, depicted a gleaming rifle, pointing outwards. Of course everyone who knows the difficulty of obtaining domestic staff will sympathise with my uncle's wife. And, I repeat, her personal loyalty remained unchanged. To this day almost every foot of wall space in her private rooms are dutifully covered with an Uncle Hamish portrait.

But I must curtail my enthusiasm and leave to posterity a fuller and more permanent study of the work of my Uncle Hamish. He is undoubtedly a painter of great originality. One might almost venture to say that he is, in his own peculiar way, a painter of genius. I like to think of him as the founder of an 'Originalist' School of Painting, a prophet before his time. If only his pictures could be got to the public or even the public got to his pictures I feel sure a most profound impression would be made. Or, failing that, even if his younger colleagues could be induced to make a study of his work, its influence upon them might well prove incalculable. But the time, obviously, is not yet ripe for such a happy twist of Fate. At the moment, Fate turns her head resolutely the other way. Only the other day several great crates arrived back from the RA, marked rejected. They were some of my uncle's greatest masterpieces. *Beak*, a colourful study of a parrot's beak, twelve feet long by seven feet high, is fit to rank with anything of its kind, in my opinion. Likewise *Sand*, a still-life view of sand – just sand, sand, sand, one vast canvas of golden sand, silent and mysterious, its implacable surface broken only in one corner by the familiar sign, Hamish I. Even *Zum-Zum*, an impression in no less than eighteen shades of the big toe of a negro jitterbug dancer – one of those extremely futuristic studies by my uncle which do not give to me quite the sense of mystic ecstasy that I find in his more traditional work – even *Zum-Zum*, I repeat, strikes me as incomparably superior to many contemporary paintings in like vein. However, tastes vary a good deal, nowhere perhaps more than among the RA selection committee. Excuses can be found, one way and another, for their rejection of these three.

But for the RA to return *Tomorrow*, the great climax of my Uncle Hamish's career – a picture on which he worked, on and off, for ten years, a picture that is truly an epic of its time – that they, miserable selection committee members, should reject this work of Great Art – that is too much. I am forced to ask myself whether there is not more in this behaviour than meets the eye. Can it be that the RA are afraid of facing reality? Can it be that they are part of a conspiracy to prevent the British public from seeing what lies ahead? That is the impression I reluctantly form ... And yet, I ask myself, why? Nothing could be more expressive. No one can ever have reduced the problems of the universe to such a simple, human and understandable level as my Uncle Hamish has achieved with his canvas *Tomorrow*. It stands before me now, filling the whole length of the drawing-room, dominating the whole scene – as, of course, is only right. Into this single canvas my Uncle

Hamish with his peculiar genius has contrived to pack every detail of past history – every evolution, revolution and devolution. Nothing has been omitted. He spent months and months in museums swotting up Roman History, Grecian History, the Ice Age and the Stone Age and even the pre-human age. In one way or another, it is his proud claim, every generation, every decade even, is represented on the canvas. The Picts by a pict axe, the Romans by a sword, the Saxons by an arrow piercing an eye (*deriv. Harold*), the Welsh by a leek, the Scots by a bagpipe, on and on ... right up to appropriate symbols of the modern age, such as machine-guns, bomber planes, flying bombs and gas-masks. The intricate detail of these items, down to the last notch of the machine gun, the whites of an eye, the leaves of a leek, would amaze you – if you could see them. In point of fact, you do not see them. That is the final master-stroke, which in many ways convinces me once and for all that my uncle really is a genius. For, as my uncle points out, the subject of the picture is *Tomorrow*. Consequently all that is left of the canvas are some frayed edges still clinging to the inside corners of the frame. (The frame, I might add, is a beautiful one of woven gold braiding. My uncle explains that this represents the peaceful hemispheres and stratospheres.) Across where the canvas should be there stretch one or two criss-crossing lengths of barbed wire. Exactly in the centre are two words daubed on a scrap of paper: *BOMBED OUT*. My uncle, nothing if not thorough, worked out the total tonnage of bombs required. But as he admits, he may be a little pessimistic. He's a painter, not a politician.

XI

A Visit to the Isles

Her name was Jackie and she had about her the slightly elfin
charm of a boy, short-cropped black hair tucked behind a neat
green beret; she looked rather what she was, a girl from the
suburban safety of Surbiton, with a regular five day week stint
as a shorthand typist up in the City; and yet here she was,
somehow out of character, stepping off the night train from
London, at the end of its long journey under the smutty dome
of Penzance Station.

And what's more, after a hasty breakfast at a local cafe,
heading along the quayside for the large white and yellow
steamer that sailed at half past nine every morning for the
Scilly Isles, some forty miles westwards ...

What had made her do so such a thing? She had asked
herself the question a dozen times during the long, rather
lonely journey down, hunched up in a corner and trying to
sleep, for all the sleepers had been booked long before by
people who planned their affairs more logically. There had
been nothing at all logical or calculated about her journey. She
had been standing on the platform at Surbiton waiting to catch
the 8.27 train to Waterloo, just as she did every morning of the
week. It was true the sun had been shining bright with all the
promise of a glorious summer's day which she knew she must
spend inside one of those new glass-houses which architects
liked to sanctify under the name of 'new modern office units'
... but it hadn't been just the sunshine which had made up her
mind. No, it had been the sudden awareness of the people
around, the men standing almost in uniform rows, every one
almost unfailingly wearing his soldier's bowler – above all the
knowledge that within a few minutes she would be jammed
together with a dozen or so of these individuals, in a seat if she

was lucky, but even then suffering the twin agonies of someone's newspaper stuck in her face, and probably an ebony umbrella handle poking her in the ribs. And then when along with the others she was disgorged at Waterloo the whole process to be repeated all over again en route for the City ...

Yes, all these things had a great deal to do with Jackie suddenly turning on her heel and walking away from the platform and out of Surbiton station, just as her customary train rattled into position ... but there was something else too. There *must* be to explain this whole contrary crazy business – rushing into Kingston and buying some summer clothes, ringing the office to explain that she was not well and would take a week of leave due to her, making hasty arrangements to stop the milk and newspapers being delivered to her tiny bachelor flat on the third floor of an old converted mansion – finally rushing up by evening train to London.

But what? She booked her ticket to St Mary's, walked up the steep gang-plank and found herself a comfortable position near the high bow – and was still sitting there, wondering about it all, when the steamer hooted three times, the gangway was trundled back and slowly, as the ropes were untied, the big boat began backing away from the long quay. A few minutes later it had turned full circle and was heading across Mount's Bay on the first stage of the three hour journey to the magical land of Lyonesse.

It was when the *Scillonian* finally reached the enchanted islands, weaving round Penninis Point and then into St Mary's harbour, that Jackie began to realise the enormity of her action. At a time when normally she would be covering up her typewriter in readiness for slipping to the Kardomah for a snack lunch – here she was standing on the busy little quayside of Hugh Town approximately three hundred and thirty miles away from her familiar office. With no clear idea of what she was going to do, or even where she was going to stay.

Well, at least she could tackle the last problem. She began walking down the tiny main street, past the gaily decorated Mermaid pub, looking for the little 'Bed and Breakfast' cards in the windows of the neat little houses. After spying several of these and knocking, only to be told regretfully that there were no vacancies and she was unlikely to find a room anywhere at this time of the year, Jackie began to lose a little of her rather artificial confidence.

She was standing in the middle of the road, looking as she felt, thoroughly disconsolate and weary, when she became conscious of someone at her side, exuding a certain warming sympathy. Looking up she saw an incredibly tanned young man in jeans and an old green sweater, with a mop of curly black hair and a friendly grin. On the back of his head he wore a battered old sailor's cap perched at a rakish angle.

'Excuse me – but you look as if you've lost something!'

Jackie could not help smiling.

'I haven't found something – put it like that.'

She went on to explain her predicament and at first the young man, who introduced himself as Joe, shook his head rather gloomily. Then suddenly he brightened.

'You'll never find anywhere here – but you'd maybe get fixed up on our island.'

'Where's that?'

'It's one of the smaller islands – not so many visitors get over there. I know one or two folk who can probably fix you up.'

Jackie looked at Joe, trying to simulate a feeling of doubt or at least hesitation, but somehow she felt a complete sense of trust in that open sunny countenance.

'Well – I suppose I haven't much choice.'

She paused.

'But how will we get there?'

Joe grinned.

'In my boat of course.'

A few moments later, after precariously climbing down one or the iron ladders on the quayside, Jackie found herself sitting nervously in the prow of a small dinghy while Joe squatted at the back operating a tiny but effective outboard motor. With a sudden zoom and roar they turned outwards and were soon humming out of the harbour and across towards distant white-sanded shores. As they went Joe began telling her, in his slow rather engaging way, that having a boat was almost an everyday custom on the islands – almost everyone he knew had a boat of some size or another. It was so to speak a way of life.

Jackie sat back, listening with one ear – but in reality her attention was elsewhere, with the sea all around her, studded here and there with the green and golden-white outline of little islands. It was incredibly peaceful and remote and soothing ... she felt as if she might be at the very end of the earth. Perhaps in a way she was.

'Well,' said Joe cheerfully, breaking across her day-dreams. 'Here we are.'

It didn't take Joe long to get Jackie fixed up for board and lodging at Mrs Curnow's little grey cottage near the quay. Jackie liked Mrs Curnow, a rosy cheeked Cornishwoman who kept her house trim and pretty, with tropical plants growing in profusion in the garden.

But then, she found, she liked a great many things about the easy, unhurried way of life of which she now found herself a part. If she had wanted to find the most precise contrast to her normal everyday life she could hardly have found a better example. Walking along the leafy lanes that led from the quayside up through the subtropical vegetation it was such an event to meet another person that it became second nature to stop and pass the time of the day ... and in the course of such conversations, mysteriously, Jackie found herself establishing a kind of contact that would not have seemed possible in Surbiton.

On the second day, after being almost pointedly left to her own resources, she found Joe sitting on the wall at the bottom of Mrs Curnow's garden.

'Hullo, there.' He grinned his broad, friendly grin. 'I'm just going fishing. Like to come?'

They chugged out in the little dinghy, passing between two steep craggy rocks and out into the deeper waters. Although sheltered, the sea swept along in steady swells that lifted the tiny boat up and down like a cork, but with Joe in charge Jackie felt quite safe. There was something timeless and peaceful about the experience; the restless sea, the murmuring wind, the cawking seagulls – the whole afternoon. Jackie shot one or two looks at Joe: he seemed absorbed in his task of laying out the lines, every movement a slow but deliberate one. She tried to imagine him in some other setting, in a big city for instance, but somehow it was impossible.

'Tell me, Joe,' she said. 'Have you lived here all your life?'

Joe paused from playing out his net and looked at her quizzically.

'Yes. All my life.'

'But – how do you make a living?'

He looked at her in genuine surprise.

'Oh, I manage. A little fishing, some boats trips in the summer, flower picking in the early spring … it's not bad.'

Everything, Jackie found, seemed to take place in the same casual manner. That afternoon a neighbour came over to ask Joe to give a hand with getting in the potatoes – Jackie went along too, and soon there were a dozen people working in a long line down the narrow field. It didn't really seem to matter whose potato crop it was – for that moment, it was the responsibility of everyone.

That was the way, she discovered, most of the life of the island went on. There were very few rules or regulations, if only because they would have seemed superfluous. If anyone needed a helping hand, somehow, mysteriously, it was offered. If it was a case of illness then there was always someone ready to come and help, or run errands for the sick person. If the illness was serious enough to warrant a special trip by one of the big launches to St Mary's and the hospital there, then there would be quick arrangements made for looking after any children or other dependants.

In the evenings, after sharing a meal with Mrs Curnow and her husband, who worked on the estate, Jackie got in the habit of strolling down the sandy lane that followed the harbour and led eventually to the island's only pub. Only it wasn't like the pubs she had known before, all glittering chrome and leather-plush; it was more like someone's parlour. Everyone seemed to know one another, just like members of a family. Joe would usually be sitting in his regular corner, and somehow always with a seat beside him waiting for her. Through Joe she met some of the other islanders – Tom Row, another fisherman, his brother Alfred, old Elias Penberthy and his wife, Maria, who farmed a smallholding on the south side, and the Tonkin brothers, who ran the island's regular launch service to St Mary's. The latter both had enormous bushy black beards and soon Jackie was teasing them about being pirates.

'Ah, no,' said one of the brothers, more seriously than Jackie had expected. ''Tisn't us that do be pirates – but some of the folk up your way, I reckon. You should see some of the prices we have to pay to get anything down.'

Jackie felt in some way bound to protest, but even as she did so she had an uneasy sense that her sympathies really lay with the black-bearded brother – who was already, curiously, more real to her than many of her neighbours in Surbiton.

That evening when she walked back from the pub with Joe at her side she said suddenly.

'Have you ever thought of leaving the island, Joe? I mean, going to live somewhere on the mainland – London perhaps?'

She supposed at first Joe thought she was joking for his blue eyes crinkled and he began to laugh. But when he realised that perhaps she was being serious his eyes narrowed and his mouth went into an unfamiliar grim line.

'No, Jackie,' he said curtly. 'Never given it a thought.'

Jackie's first reaction was a kind of anger. Who was Joe to think with such superiority about himself and his precious island? What right had he to assume so much ...? Her anger lasted sufficiently to goad her into bidding Joe a very curt goodnight and leaving him standing on the doorstep, looking rather puzzled.

But later, when she was snuggled up in the old fashioned bed in Mrs Curnow's that night she found herself thinking a little differently. She remembered a walk they had taken that afternoon, up out of the village and on to the heather-strewn moor. There, standing like some ancient sentinel were the ruins of an old castle: she and Joe had wandered in and climbed to the parapet to look out over a panoramic view of the islands. It was a beautiful and even majestic sight, the glittering blue sea studded with dozens and dozens of tiny islands. It was very much like a whole universe. What more could anyone want?

The next day when she wandered down to the little quay she was curiously hurt to find Joe's boat gone, and to be told by one of the old men who sat on the wall smoking a pipe that he had gone fishing. Despite herself Jackie could not resist walking along the cliff-path that wound out towards the point – from there she had a clear view of Joe's tiny blue and white boat, bobbing up and down at anchor just off the point while he tended his lines. Watching, taking in the utterly tranquil scene, she felt a sudden unexpected pang at the thought: soon I must leave it all.

Yet somehow by the time she next encountered Joe, not altogether by accident, for she watched his boat heading home and happened to be sitting on the quay just by where he would land – she found herself arguing again in the same way.

'... I'm surprised you haven't more spirit of adventure about you. The whole world outside waiting to be explored ...'

Joe looked at her patiently.

'It really depends what you want out of life, doesn't it?'

She pouted, unexpectedly goaded by what she regarded as his complacency.

'Well, thank goodness, not everyone's in a groove!'

He inclined his head.

'Never mind – you'll be well out of it soon, won't you?'

Jackie stiffened.

'Yes thank you very much – I will. As a matter of fact I plan to go back tomorrow. I think I've been here long enough.'

She could have bitten her tongue off the moment the words were out, but by then it was too late, and pride compelled her to fulfil the promise. She explained her decision to Mrs Curnow, who didn't help matters by spending the rest of the evening trying to persuade her to stay.

'No, really, I can't,' she said with a resolution she did not really feel. 'I must get back, I really must.' And as she spoke she had a fleeting, rather dismal, view of the return to routine, the 8.27 train again, the tube to the City, the climb up the subway, the entry into the chromium plated hall of the office ...

In the morning she ate hardly any breakfast, then packed her things into her single case and went down to the quay to catch the motor launch that ran every day to connect with the *Scillonian*. Before she could reach the quay, however, she was stopped by the sudden appearance of Joe, looking rather sheepish.

'It's all right – I'll run you across.'

Pride prodded her to refuse, but fortunately some other stronger feeling impelled her to acquiesce, if a little grudgingly. Joe took her case and led the way across the sand to where his boat was moored. She climbed in and Joe gave a push to get the boat afloat, then jumped in. He swung once or twice at the cord which started the outboard engine, and soon it was humming away and they were heading – for the last time, she thought sadly – out down the channel.

For a long time neither of them spoke. They sat like two strangers, Joe at the stern, one hand resting on the rudder, Jackie up in the prow. All around them the waters of the Sound were as still as a mill pond, the only disturbance being the frothing wake of the little motor boat. Looking around Jackie was surprised to feel tiny tears pricking at the back of her eyes as she thought: *I shall never know this sort of peace again.*

Then, just as she was wondering if she could hold back the tears any longer, there was a spluttering sound – and the engine suddenly cut out.

Joe bent down and fiddled with the cord, pulling it once, twice, three times, without result.

'What is it?' she said.

'I don't know – maybe it's the carburettor. I'll just check.'

She sat irresolutely at the back of the boat, now bobbing gently up and down, while Joe huddled over the engine, screwing and unscrewing various nuts and bolts. Jackie looked at her watch: it was now only about quarter of an hour before the *Scillonian* was due to sail.

At last Joe sat back shrugging his shoulders.

'It's no good … I can't get it to work.'

'But …' Jackie opened her arms helplessly. 'What about the steamer? I'll miss it.' She looked around. 'Can't you row or something?'

Joe avoided her eyes.

'I, er, forgot to bring the oars … It's usually so reliable you see.'

'Oh, really!'

Jackie looked around, suddenly alarmed.

'Look, we're drifting …'

Joe followed her gaze dutifully, and nodded.

'Yes, that's right. It's the current, you see. It'll carry us along to the west.'

Jackie followed the direction of his pointing hand.

'But – but that's taking us back to the island.'

Joe averted his eyes.

'Yes, I guess so.'

But here they were both wrong. Some quirk in the tides took them a great deal wider than might have been imagined, with the result that the little blue dinghy drifted right past the tip of the island and they were carried on about half a mile towards one of the smaller, uninhabited islands.

'At least it was inhabited once,' said Joe thoughtfully seemingly quite unperturbed by their possible fate. 'But the people gave up – there's just the shell of one or two houses. But it's a lovely little place – quite sheltered, too. And a wonderful beach – just look at it.'

Jackie reflected that she was going to have plenty of time to look at the beach as their boat drifted directly up to the long white shoal, until the prow sank into the shallow sand. They were still several yards from dry land, Joe got out in his wading boots and held out his arms.

'Come on. I'll carry you.'

It was not at all how Jackie had imagined spending that particular morning – she knew she should by rights have been on the big steamer whose disappearing shape she could just see on the horizon – but the curious thing was that she rather enjoyed the sensation of being borne off and deposited on the bare white sands, rather as if she had been captured by some pirate chief and taken to his lair. Come to think of it, in his jerkin and jeans and with his peaked cap perched on the back of his head, Joe did look rather piratical.

'Well,' she said, when they were sitting side by side on the beach, looking at the boat as it rocked innocently on the edge, 'What do we do now? Wave a white flag or light a flare or something?'

'Oh, no,' said Joe cheerfully. 'I expect I'll be able to get the engine going all right a bit later …'

'That's all very well,' began Jackie, 'but now I've missed the boat –'

Suddenly she stopped, catching an unfamiliar glint in Joe's eyes. Suspicion that had lurked suddenly solidified into certainty.

'Oh, no! It's not possible!' She glared at Joe. '*You* made the engine break down.'

Joe looked up at the sky, across the water, into the sea – finally, a little uneasily, he met Jackie's accusing gaze.

'Er, well … yes, I suppose I did. You see –'

But Jackie did not want to see. She felt all kind of pent-up anger and frustration welling up until she could contain them no longer, and with a sharp cry she threw herself upon the surprised Joe, pushing him over, and banging on his chest with her fists.

'How dare you! I hate you! You're a vile, beastly –'

But somehow she could not keep up her protesting for long – somehow she knew, with sudden certainty, that she was glad about the engine breakdown, glad she would miss the boat – above all glad that she was here now with Joe, dear lovable Joe – who must surely love her indeed.

And so her visit to the isles went on and on … and on. And they both lived happily ever afterwards.

XII

Christmas Story

The enormous balloon came floating down the main street at about four o'clock in the afternoon, bobbing above the anonymous heads of the bustling worrying crowd – up-down, hu-up-down, hup-down, a vast red and blue balloon, decorated with a huge white outline of Father Christmas, and perched on the end of a long thin stick.

Attached to the stick was the aching hand of an earnest young man wearing a new grey macintosh. He might have been a clerk or a shop assistant, or maybe a minor civil servant or any other kind of young man travelling home from work … except for the huge balloon.

After a while, waving his hand about dramatically in order to avoid poking the stick into people's eyes or the balloon through a shop window, the young man joined a bus queue. In this stood a phlegmatic cross-section of the city's citizens: short men and long tall men, fat ladies and thin ladies, young cheeky office boys and old grumbly grandfathers – all pre-occupied and morose, all weighed down by the terrible cares of the world. Not one of them, as it happened, carried a balloon.

At first the young man tried to pretend it was an everyday event for him to be standing there holding a large red and blue balloon. He hummed a tune, he looked round airily, he peered around him for sight of a bus.

Then, unnervingly, he encountered a pair of steely grey eyes on him with what he took to be an accusing look. In fact their owner was probably trying to remember the time of an appointment, or maybe the recipe for an evening meal: but to the young man the look spelt out condemnation, and he rushed, to defend himself.

'Pretty, isn't it? The balloon, I mean. Rather a silly idea, I suppose. I mean ... well, to tell you the truth, I don't quite know how it happened. You see, Mary, that's my wife, she said, we could do with a balloon or two for Christmas, and then I was walking along and – well, there this was, hanging outside a shop, a real stopper. So I went in and bought it.'

The young man paused for breath, and looked round even more defiantly.

'She's three, my little girl. And mad about balloons. You see –'

Suddenly his words fell on emptiness. The bus had arrived, the queue poured aboard as if carried by some relentless conveyor belt.

'Hey!' cried the young man, quite angrily, and he plunged into the mêlée, squashing his clothes but somehow managing to preserve the balloon – up and over, past the severely critical eyebrows-raised-high look of the conductor, and into the long, narrow heaving jungle of the lower deck.

'Phew!' exclaimed the young man, mopping his forehead. He was standing, of course, third in a row. Now, as the bus started with a vicious jerk, the whole row was thrown off balance. Despairingly, the young man grabbed for a steel pillar.

Free, the balloon floated away and along the bus until it came to rest in the lap of a stout lady with a detached, aristocratic look. She continued to stare out of the window as if by so doing she would in some way preserve a world in which there just was *not* a Christmas balloon on her lap.

Discreetly, even timorously, the young man leaned over and took back his balloon.

But a moment later came another lurch and again the young man had to grab for support. This time the balloon, after balancing miraculously for several moments on the round egg-head of a bald gentleman, slid into the expectant waiting grasp of a talkative type.

Here, obviously, was a ready humorist. Gleefully he held up the balloon for all to see.

'Well, ladies and gentlemen, and what have we here? A bargain if ever I saw one. Well, now who'll buy my nice balloon? Sold – sold to the gentleman on my right there.'

And with a deft pat he sent the great balloon sailing past the young man's out-stretched hand and into the astonished grasp

of a middle-aged clerk. With the balloon the wit must have
passed over some of his abundant liveliness, for no sober clerk
in his right mind would then have leaned forward – as this one
now did – and blow – yes, playfully blow – the balloon into
the pretty face of a young typist.

'I say – really, I say – it's my balloon!' protested the young
man to all and sundry.

But perhaps the typist didn't hear him. Enough to say, she
had a mischievous tilt to her lips and a bright gleam in her
dark eyes: hardly surprising, really, that with a delicious pout
she lifted up the balloon and – whoosh!' – it went sailing right
across the bus.

Too late now for the young man to gesticulate and open his
mouth. Nobody would have heard him for the rumble of
sound that swept around. An elderly gent in the back
sportingly gave the balloon a tap with his spectacle case: a deft
office boy gave it a helping hand; and in no time at all the
balloon was being smacked backwards and forwards, to the
accompaniment of hilarious shouts.

'Now, now, what's going on?' demanded the conductor,
rattling his ticket bag angrily. 'You can't carry on like this –
what d'you think this is, a playground?'

He moved imperiously down the bus, quelling the
momentary riot with the authority of his uniform, his badge,
his peaked cap – above all, his inhibiting up-and-down
eyebrows.

'And what may this be?' said the conductor, witheringly,
retrieving the balloon from a humble company director who, a
few seconds before, had been about to clout it for six.

Feeling himself suddenly the centre of an Incident, the
young man shrivelled up.

'It's a – it's *mine*,' he said, in a stage whisper.

'Oh,' said the conductor, sarcastically. 'So it's yours, is it?
Well, just see that you look after it, see? Balloons, indeed. I've
a good mind to charge you a fare for it, at that.'

Martinet-like, he glared around the bus, as if daring any
rebellious spirit to declare itself.

'Come along now, then – fares please.'

Before the onslaught of authority, like a pack of small
children, the passengers subsided into a guilty silence. And yet,

as the conductor moved around, a subtle conspiracy of mirth emerged. The humorist looked over at the clerk and gave a broad wink ... the clerk smiled politely at the typist ... she smiled roguishly at someone else ... somehow you could almost feel the silent ripples of laughter spreading around.

At first, still standing, cringing away from the formidable conductor while at the same time holding his balloon well out of reach of a large hat-pin fixed in the hair of a lady in the seat below him – the young man did not notice the atmosphere.

Then, slowly, its warmth began to penetrate ... Nervously, then with growing confidence, he began to look around. Everywhere there were eyes waiting to catch his, smiles at the ready, friendly nods. When the conductor had finished and returned to his platform, and there was more room to move, the young man felt himself positively expanding with the glow of good fellowship.

At last he felt compelled to make some comment.

'Silly idea, I suppose you're thinking. But you know what kids are like. I can't help thinking she'll get a lot of fun this Christmas, don't you agree?'

Nobody answered directly. But somehow there was a sort of answer in the air, warm and cheery, a curious sense of companionship, which quite touched the young man, so that he nearly missed his stop.

When he got out, awkwardly, still clutching his balloon, and then set off rather unsteadily down the road, it seemed as if the whole busful of people turned to watch him. Indeed, they stared after him almost hungrily, as if they didn't want to lose him completely, as if they wanted somehow to savour his existence to the very last drop.

And long after the conductor had pressed the button and the bus drove away – indeed right until they had reached their holly and mistletoe decorated homes and were sitting by their fires, remembering to their families, 'I must tell you, what happened today on the bus, there was a young man with a big Christmas balloon', – they were surprised to find themselves feeling curiously happy, and just for a time almost unworried by all the world's cares.

As for the young man, as he turned the key in the lock and opened the door and went into the delightful familiarity of his own home, he felt elevated, distinguished, triumphant – victor as it were of some tremendous campaign.

'Hullo, darling,' he called out to his wife. 'Well, I *remembered*.'

And as he entered he brandished high the bright red and blue balloon with the puffed out white shape of Father Christmas.

And the little girl played with it happily ever afterwards.

XIII

Mist

Philip Anderson arrived back in England, toughened and suntanned after many years cattle-farming in Australia, filled with a single dominating thought – to get down to the family farm in Cornwall and square accounts with his elder brother, Ben.

It was Ben who had stayed to help their ailing father run the farm and who had now inherited the farm after their father's sudden death. And it was Ben, in Philip's opinion, who must have been responsible for that death. For otherwise how could their father have lost his life out on a moor which he knew like the back of his hand? He had been found dead at the bottom of a thirty foot drop into an old quarry working. It must have been the sea mist, Ben had written in explanation.

Back on the farm, surrounded by familiar reminders of childhood days, Philip recognised the temptation to settle down as if nothing had happened – indeed Ben offered him a permanent home if he cared to stay. But Philip refused angrily.

For a week or two the brothers went their ways, Ben carrying on the farmwork, his brother wandering up on the moors. One day Philip decided to make a trip in the footsteps of his father's last journey. When he started the sun was beating down but as Philip climbed higher the heat faded until when he looked back he found the farm hidden by the greyness of a mist that had crept in from the Atlantic ocean.

It had often been his experience, in the old days, to see the mist covering the level bend below, and then disappear as mysteriously as it had appeared. He did not therefore, worry unduly, but went on his way, climbing between great boulders and over clumps of blue heather, following the wandering footpath that he knew crossed the whole moor before leading down to a cluster of cottages on the other side.

It was about half an hour later when he stopped and looked down at his feet almost shocked to find them half enveloped in the grey, puffy fingers of the mist. Looking around, he saw that it had crept steadily upwards, until it had engulfed not only the land below but the edges of the moor itself. And now it hung all around him, silent, somehow rather menacing – just as that other day it must have gathered around his doomed father.

Stifling a feeling of fear, Philip went doggedly on his way. He would follow the path, come what may, mist or no mist. That alone would prove that his father's death had been due to no accident.

Now, as he walked, the mist swirled higher and higher, sometimes reaching up so that the damp prickle caught at his throat, and he coughed and spluttered, it was certainly an eerie feeling to be so surrounded, he could not remember an experience like it before: It was rather as if the mist had some evil aim, as if it was motivated, purposeful, an enemy. How grey and thick it had become, how huge and dark, hanging around him like some enormous great cloud difficult to believe that a world existed beyond, a world of light and life. Here there was only brooding silence, and mist everywhere.

Shivering, Philip plodded on, his shoulders hunched, his eyes staring blindly into the mist ahead. On and on and on – and then suddenly, shocked, he stopped. Intuitively, he knew that he was no longer on the path. He had been following it closely, he had never for a second taken his eyes off the slender track or so it seemed. And yet he peered around: here was no path, he was walking over rubble and heather-strewn wilderness.

For the first time he admitted to the fear that he had felt at the back of his mind. He had been out on the moor at night before, and never felt this fear. At night there was always a distant light to guide you home, or at the worst, the charitable stars. But now, although it was daytime, the moor was far worse than any night. The mist obliterated everything – not only the light, the path, but the world, the sense of being part of human existence.

Here one was alone completely alone, and yet not alone. For all around there gathered weird shapes of mist. At least, they seemed of mist. But perhaps they were something more. Perhaps … ?

It was then that Philip began to lose his nerve. In desperation he began crying out: 'Hullo! Help! Help!' But even his voice seemed muffled and lost in this overwhelming, awful mist. Still impelled by a sense of self-preservation, he went on crying out, forlornly, despairingly.

Remembering past advice, he knew that the most sensible thing to do would be to stand still, to wait until the mist lifted. And yet, fear would not let him be still, fear compelled him to walk on, even into the unknown hoping to come back to the path. Fear guided him on, into the heart of the mist. He could not see more than an inch or two ahead of him, the mist was all around, damp on his face, heavy on his clothes. And still he called out, 'Help! Help!'

Then suddenly, miraculously, he heard an answering cry. It came from somewhere behind. It was the voice of his brother, Ben – it entreated him to stand still, not to move another foot.

After what seemed an eternity, Ben loomed out of the mist. His face was anxious he reached out a hand and took Philip's elbow.

'Thank God – I was afraid,' his brother's voice tailed off, but Philip looked in his eyes and knew what he meant. Slowly he put out his hand and clasped his brother's. 'I guessed you had made up your mind to take the same walk, and I feared the same result.'

'It was like this, the night father died?'

'Yes, Philip. Like this but even worse. I searched for hours. I wandered all over the place, it was terrible, like being lost at sea.' Ben's voice had a catch in it suddenly. 'I don't think I shall ever be able to forget that night …'

Suddenly Philip was filled with shame, and with pity for his brother. He realised just what he must have gone through, alone in this terrible mist searching without cease, yet never finding – until too late. He saw now how easy it would have been for his father – indeed for himself had not Ben heard his cries – to have fallen into the quarry. It would have been impossible to see the edges until it was too late, until your feet were already giving way.

'Ben,' he said at last. 'Do we have a chance of getting back?'

His brother smiled.

'I brought a handful of white stones in my pocket. I've been dropping them as I went. Yes, we'll get back …'

Hand in hand the two brothers set off through the mist. It seemed an interminable journey, yet together they did not feel afraid.

When finally they were safely back at the farm Philip looked at his brother shyly.

'Ben, I've been thinking – I'd like to stay on, after all.'

XIV

The Tune

Da-da-di-da-di-da – da –

It went something like that, the tune. At least, that's how Benson said it went. He used to hum it over and over again.

Da-da-di-da-di-da – da –

Hmmmmh. Yes. I can remember – well, yes, I suppose I can remember from the very beginning, from the time Benson first heard the tune. Before that, you see, Benson was just an ordinary sort of fellow, sober, neatly dressed, regular in his habits ... We shared an office in the same business house. Every morning at about the same time we would arrive from our different homes, our different directions, our different ways of life – and then for eight hours or so we were together, sharing not only an office but most of the day's events. Sometimes we might have outside luncheon appointments, but if not we often shared a sandwich and a can of beer. That's when we used to talk a little, not exactly intimately, but with a certain closeness. He came to know that I was a family man, glad to get back to my wife and children and my snug little home. I learned that Benson was something of a confirmed bachelor, living an ordered, regular somewhat dull sort of life. He seemed a pleasant, rather self-effacing sort of fellow, a life devoid of drama, until –

Well, until I first began to notice his new, unfamiliar air of tension. A sort of tightening of the skin, a nervousness of movement – above all a strange, haunted kind of look in his eyes. It was impossible not to notice the difference; usually Benson was stolid, almost phlegmatic, a man of plodding method and routine.

Now, suddenly, he was all nervy and jumpy, taking to padding about the office like the proverbial cat on hot bricks.

I didn't say anything at first. I mean, office acquaintanceship has its limits, one doesn't like to intrude into people's private lives. I used to watch him, though, sometimes, and I found it curiously disturbing. He seemed, somehow, to be withdrawn into himself – to be trying to forget about his immediate surroundings. It was almost as if – well, yes, studying the expression on his face, I could not help feeling this – it was almost as if he were listening to something. Or trying to, anyway.

I kept my peace for quite a long time, and all the time Benson seemed to grow more and more introspective, more and more – well, I suppose one could only say peculiar. I don't think anyone else noticed it because no one else spent so much time alone with the man. But I could not help notice, and in the end I felt I had to say something.

One day when he was slumped in his chair, staring out of the window – and yet somehow, I knew, *not really* staring out of the window – I coughed, and leaned forward.

'I say, old chap – are you all right? Is anything – wrong?'

Benson started. For a moment his eyes, as they turned to me, were almost wild looking, before he seemed to come back to reality. When he spoke, it was rather wanly, with the ghost of a smile.

'Sorry. I was – well, never mind. What was it you wanted?'

I hesitated. But he looked so miserable, so inwardly distraught, I had to press on.

'I was a little worried. You seemed – well, upset. I've noticed lately. Are you feeling all right? Anything worrying you?'

Benson looked at me curiously.

'So you've noticed. Yes, I suppose you would ...'

Then all at once he suddenly started up, and half held his hand up as if for silence. I watched him amazed. He was not looking at me any more, he was looking away – he seemed to be straining – yes, straining to catch something, some sound, some echo.

'There,' he said suddenly. 'There – can you hear?'

Suddenly his eyes were fixed on me, but with a rather frightening intensity – almost an appeal.

'Surely – surely you can hear?'

'Hear?' I looked at him blankly. 'Hear what?'

I shall never forget the look in Benson's eyes that afternoon when he comprehended the meaning of my answer. I realised afterwards that it was the first time he had dared to ask that question. And my answer, confirming all his secret fears, must have seemed like – well like a kind of death-knell.

'What is it?' I asked. 'What is it you can hear?'

Benson gave a little groan, and held his head between his hands. At least that is what it seemed to be at first – but at last I realised he was doing something else. He was covering his ears with his hands, pressing them tightly against the apertures.

I became alarmed, and came over to stand by him.

'Benson ... are you sure you're all right?'

He looked up at me wearily.

'You don't hear anything? Nothing at all?'

I stood and listened. Everything was still, the only sound I could remotely hear was of the traffic outside.

'No,' Benson shook his head. 'I don't mean the traffic. I mean ...'

He hesitated, as if trying not to give way: and then with a violence that was frightening, began to pound his ears.

'I mean that tune – that damned, terrible tune!'

I had never seen a man give way to an obsession before, and I was quite frightened. But I felt it was my duty to try and help Benson.

'There's no tune,' I said gently. 'Really. I can't hear anything. You must be –'

I suppose Benson knew the easy soothing words I was about to utter, and despised me for them. He jumped to his feet and began walking about the office.

'You don't understand. I'm not imagining things. I *can* hear a tune. I can hear it quite distinctly.' He paused and looked at me with unmistakable anguish. 'I've been hearing it now for days and days – oh, God, yes, and for nights and nights, too.' He winced, and shuddered. 'The awful thing is – I can hear it now, too – this very moment.'

He paused and stood there: and I knew then, fearfully, that indeed he could hear something. His whole bearing, his whole being, was given up to the act of listening.

'Yes,' said Benson at last, controlling himself a little. 'I can hear the tune quite clearly. It goes like this.'

And he began to hum it to me.

Da-da-di-da-di-da da- Da-da-di-da-di-da-da-

'But –' I said. 'But – but –'

And then I stopped, for I didn't know what else to say. Somehow what I had seen convinced me that Benson really did hear the tune. And yet ... what could it mean? How could he hear a tune, he alone in the world? It didn't make sense.

It didn't make sense, but it did make for a sense of horror, and even despair. After breaking down like that Benson seemed almost grateful that he had found a confidant. He began to pour out his heart to me about his strange affliction. Yes, affliction, that is how I came to view it. I mean, it must have been, mustn't it?

Benson said he could not exactly remember when he first heard the tune – the trouble was now he found it impossible to remember or even to imagine a world in which there was not this tune for background. Now he heard it nearly all the time.

'Sometimes at night I finally drop off into a half-sleep – and then all at once I wake up – indeed, I am awakened – because the tune is ringing in my ears. Oh, you've no idea how awful it is – how terrible. I get no peace – no peace at all.'

I could see that it was beginning to affect Benson's health, quite apart from his work. I said he ought to go and see a doctor. He shook his head.

'You don't understand. I've been to doctors. They can't help me. They don't understand ...'

It was then, I think, that I had some inkling of the inevitability of Benson's tragedy. He was a man sliding to doom, and he knew it.

'It's getting worse,' he said, coming in white-faced one morning. 'Horrible ... It's getting louder. Louder and louder ... so that I can hardly hear anything else.'

In vain did I question him, try and pin him down to what I imagined to be reality.

'But what does it sound like – I mean what kind of sound do you hear?'

He just shook his head.

'I can't begin to tell you. It's just noise – a sound – a tune, volume, rising – it's everywhere all around.'

He looked at me a little wildly.

'Don't you understand! – it's here, in this room. It exists – it's waiting, waiting to be heard. I *know* …'

And then he raised his hands in that familiar, helpless gesture, to try and shut out the tune that would not be shut out.

I must confess it was beginning to get me down. I even contemplated trying to get a transfer to another office, but somehow I felt that would be unfair to Benson, somehow letting him down. So I stayed on there, day after day listening to his terrible tales, learning how the tune was assuming monstrous volumes in his life, trying to comfort him against I knew not what fate.

At last, blessed relief, came the holiday period. For two whole weeks I would be away not only from the office, but from Benson.

I looked at him curiously on the last day.

'Well, I hope you have a change and a rest. Where are you going?'

Benson looked at me blankly. That's how he always looked nowadays, blank and drained of all life and purpose.

'Going? I – don't know. I haven't thought. I – can't think really. I can only … listen.'

I never saw him again. When I came back cheerful and refreshed from my holiday, there was an empty chair opposite me. There was no word, no message. After a day or two the company secretary rang me up and asked me if I knew what had happened to Benson. I said I had no idea … but even as I spoke, something stirred in me uneasily, a kind of premonition.

A few days later the secretary rang me back. He sounded curiously hushed and grave.

'Extraordinary thing about Benson – have you heard? He's dead.'

'Dead?' I said slowly. 'You mean he –?'

'Oh, I think it's all quite straightforward – died of a heart attack. Apparently he didn't go away or anything, just shut himself up in his digs. One morning his landlady went in and found him dead. Must have died in his sleep, they reckon.' The secretary paused. 'Funny thing, really. He wasn't that old, was he?'

I didn't bother to answer. I knew somehow that age had very little to do with Benson's death. I knew in my heart, somehow, that it must have been a death more mysterious than anyone realised.

I was right, too. I took the trouble to buy a copy of the local paper that reported the inquest on Benson. It was true enough that he died of a heart attack – but then so might you or I in all the circumstances. For at the inquest a very strange fact was recorded: when the autopsy was carried out the pathologist made an unusual discovery – *both the dead man's eardrums were broken.*

XV

The Last Laugh

Up among the hills of Penwith, although it's at the far end of Cornwall, there are cottages and farms, and even whole villages where you could live all your life without a sight of the sea – yes, and that despite the fact that the sea stretches everywhere a matter of six or seven miles away. The villages cluster into little hollows and the folds of the bare moorland hills rise all around, almost as if in protection.

Protection from what? Well, from the terrible winds that sweep in from the Atlantic, a good many folk would say. But there are other, even more terrible things against which the encircling hills might offer their shelter. The sea itself, for instance – I met a man once in one of the tiny Penwith villages who admitted quite frankly that he felt more at ease, happier indeed, because in such a remote and sheltered spot he was hidden from the sea. No, he wasn't a seaman or anything like that. But he'd had a peculiarly intimate relationship with water. I gathered that. And there were memories, unforgettable memories which somehow, I sensed, couldn't be hidden from even behind our gaunt Cornish hills.

Mind you, Howells – that was the man's name, Welsh, of course, so naturally he felt quite at home in a Celtic land like Cornwall – well, Howells had come far enough in his attempts to escape from his memories. Three hundred miles or so, in fact. And still you could see in his eyes, stolid and comfortable looking old man that he was, some flickering vision of a disturbing past.

I suppose I became rather intrigued. I was living in Penzance at the time, but often I would catch a bus out to the cross-roads, and walk half-a-mile or so down the winding valley road into the village, and up to the little pub called The

Engine Inn. Rather ironical, I thought afterwards, that old
Howells should spend his last drinking days in a pub of that
name.

We got talking over a glass of beer one day, and then we
often used to have a little chat. We became quite friendly, in
fact, so I suppose it was only natural that we should finally start
rummaging into the past. I was always a bit curious to know
just why a man like Howells, quite a town-bird in his way,
should choose to retire to such a remote spot. I think we got
around to the real heart of the matter on one occasion when I
invited him to come out with me on one of the Newlyn
pilchard fishing boats, belonging to a pal of mine. Old
Howells lifted up his sharp little head – rather like a bird's it
was – and looked quite horrified. No, he wouldn't hear of it.
Never went near the sea. Never went near water at all. Hated
the stuff.

And then, when he'd had another drink or so, he told me
why.

Before he came to Cornwall, Howells used to work in a
waterworks on the outskirts of London. He was on the
maintenance staff, night shift. Once you got used to the hours,
he said, it wasn't so bad. He used to work with a mate, a
younger man, called Chris, proper Cockney type with a sharp
tongue and lively wit. They'd go round inspecting the various
water plants, but most of the night they'd be sitting in the main
engine room where the larger turbines and the purifying
machines were pounding away.

Howells never liked the engine room from the beginning. It
was an enormous building, painted throughout a brilliant
white and flooded with highly powerful electric lighting. There
was something merciless about the lighting, he said. It seemed
to spotlight and reveal everything, so that there was no shelter
at all. Just the light and the bare white walls and the steel floors
– and the machines.

It was the machines upon which Howells' attention became
focussed. Although, officially, he was in charge of the
machines, he began to feel more and more the emptiness,
indeed the impotence, of his position. The great revolving
wheels, the plunging shining pistons, the whirring camshafts –
there was something inevitable about their movement. In all

the five years he was on night duty the machines never once stopped their relentless journey. Not until – (and there he pulled himself up, and shivered).

Sometimes he tried to explain these feeling to Chris, but he soon discovered that Chris had quite a different outlook on the machines. He used to joke about them, treat them in fact rather like a master might have treated very inferior servants in the Victorian days. His little pets, he would call the big twin-turbines, and he'd give names to some of the other enormous creations of steel. But there was something terribly contemptuous about Chris's attitude. He made it so evident that to him machines were just tools and slaves, just instruments abjectly designed to serve man's purposes.

Howells couldn't feel like that. As he sat there, night after night, lulled by the rhythmic hissing and pounding, he would often fall into a half-doze, and it was only too easy in that state to get the machines into quite a different focus. To Howells, from quite an early time, the machines were very real things, very alive things – very human things.

A silly idea perhaps? yes, that was what Chris said, when he tried to express himself to the younger man. And when he persisted, Chris pointed derisively to nuts and bolts, to wire screws, green number plates, steel bars. Could they *talk*? he would jeer. And then he'd tell Howells to stop believing in fairies, and so on.

But perhaps the machines could talk? That was the sort of idea that drifted into Howell's mind, in those nightly reveries. And, indeed, try as he would to rationalise, he couldn't help thinking that sometimes the hissing and the thumping formed into queer unrhythmical patterns – into voices.

He began to wonder if he was turning queer, then, and he was afraid to tell Chris. But somehow, almost as if for devilment, the younger man seemed to go out of his way to deride Howells' vague theories – and to ridicule the machines themselves. What were they but a lot of old junk, he scoffed. Without a man to shape and fashion them, they'd be useless. And so on.

Somehow, Howells didn't feel easy about Chris going on like this. Perhaps some sixth sense was at work on him. And then, one night – well, he could have sworn that the crashing noise of the turbines and pistons spelt out a message. Da-di-da-di-di-di-da-di-da- quite what it meant, Howells couldn't be sure. But he could have sworn – and indeed he would still swear – that the hissing undertones spat out the name 'Chris'. And there was such an underlying, concentrated venom about the sound that he found himself impelled, against his conventional judgment, to warn Chris.

Against what, jeered Chris. Against these old bits of iron? And to show what a lot of nonsense old Howells was talking he began, perversely, to taunt the machines. He began, and this frightened Howells more than anything, to treat the machines with even less respect than before – even to the extent of becoming careless in his treatment of them. There were certain regulations and safety precautions which Chris and Howells were supposed to observe – but now Chris seemed to become deliberately offhand, even reckless. And if Howells remonstrated with him, he just laughed out loud, and the laughter rose up and echoed about the white building, for a moment drowning even the sound of the machines.

It was the laughter, Howells always believed, that brought about the – happening. Chris was laughing out, loud and impudently, on that last evening. Howells tried to stop him. Something, some instinct, told him that there was something strange and sinister in the air. He could remember it now, how the building was so white and pitiless, how the lights blazed more fiercely than ever, and how, or so it seemed, the noises of the machines took on a dull, unfamiliar rumble, a rumble that beat into a steady thunder.

It was so very like a storm building up, approaching, growing in magnitude, that in a way Howells was only half surprised when the final lightning struck. Only – it wasn't lightning. No, it was one of the hydraulic-propelled pistons, a massive steel battering ram. Howells was too dazed by the thundering noise to remember exactly what happened. It did seem to him that though Chris was leaning over the safety railing, he was quite clear of the piston – and yet a moment later there was a terrible thud, and an impression of a gigantic shadow flying across the whiteness as the crumpled body was hurtled across the room and through an enormous glazed glass window, into space and eternity.

Yes, said Howells to me that evening, putting down his glass with a sigh, Chris's body was catapulted right out of the engine room – into one of the water wells. It was a nasty business fishing him out, too. That was why he never liked to go near water any more, he could only think of the water that was the last resting place of Chris.

But I could tell it wasn't really water that had scared old Howells so much. I could tell that something had happened that night, or he thought it had happened, that had shaken his whole being. Something to do with machines that became alive, and had voices – and dealt ruthlessly with their puny makers. It would be a terrifying idea, if brooded upon. You could well understand that, for a man who had been through such an experience, not even the remotest hamlet in Cornwall could really provide escape. Who knew but that behind those deceptive hills, the machines were gathering and multiplying, massing their armies for the final conquest of that fragile mankind which thought itself master – but perhaps soon would be slave.

The odd thing is that about a year later a runaway car careered down the village hill and knocked old Howells over, killing him instantly. The car – it was driverless – ran on for another quarter of a mile before finally it smashed into a stone wall. The brakes had slipped and it had rolled down the slope into the hill of its own volition. Its runaway journey was quite unpremeditated, quite purposeless. And yet – who knows?

XVI
Child of Time

1

Once upon a childhood there was a little white boy with a
mocking smile, and the memory of a wind-swept gipsy and a
soft-skinned virgin with bright black eyes ...

The little white boy was smooth and soft and could smile
with his eyes. Was his name Joseph? Or was his name Jacob?
Or had he no name, but a head and a nose and lungs and the
veins and the little white heart of a dewdrop? Was he dark of
the gipsy? Or fair of the woman? Or was he the spilt milk of a
hundred colours and the raw flesh from the hanked shafts of a
thousand million men? Was he from yesterday? Or was he
from to-morrow? Or was he from the timeless womb of the
sad lingering everydays? He was the little white boy with the
small clenched fists and the skin of a dove and never washed
cleaner than in the dew of the first morning.

He was a mocking boy with the living eyes and he was a
stubble of hairless wonder, his old bald pate a dull sadness. He
was a pummelled boy and a punched boy and a quaked,
giggling boy with the dancing fairies in his mouth. He was the
warm boy with the sucking mouth and the quick bladder, but
air cloaked the pinched shoulders and a balloon was his head.
He lay on a deep bed and the sun switched on and the air
wrapt in a parcel and poured wine over him with a tickling
gurgle. Soft-boned hands were for leaning on and the tubbed
abdomen was empty for swelling with the good blooded milk
and the bent happiness of him could lie laughing all day
without a cloud to frown the sun or a stone to drop in the still
pools outside. He rolled in the groundless soil and wrapped in
the wet laughter of nymphs and he was white without a stain,

only sprinkled with the trickling water-pearls of the morning dew.

A green field was for his head to roll upon and his dangling legs to kiss the soft moss and jump the sad-eyed cows. A hedge was the towering wall of Babylon and the green joyful forest of nowhere, with waving windows. A tree was the stonewall castle of a haunted earth bird and the sky's sentinel, stretching to the unseen winks of a dancing star. A mound of earth was a stormed mountain and a jagged rock and its weed and its dead brown grass were the sand of the seaside on a rainy afternoon. A house was the vast bees' honeycomb in a net-strewn cave and the stony steps were the winding staircase of a day's expedition. In a strawberry bed of roses the little white boy sat with a saintly smile and the far-away fields and the hidden hedges and the isolated trees and the buried mounds of earth and the sunken grey houses were lost in the yellow-tipped corners of his casual eyes.

The little white boy laughed his mocking laugh and the birds streamed across a sunlit orchard, where the aged peasant plucked a cherry tree. Ha! Ha! Ha! laughed the little white boy with his first dull tooth, and he rolled and twisted and convulsed with the joke of his whole white life. He! He! He! laughed the little white boy shining his pink bliss. One, and two, and three, and four, and five, throw away the bad one, and six and seven and eight intoned the old peasant and her torn-worn dress clung to the muddy ground where the little white boy felt her wizened legs and gazed up at the wrinkles of her hair. Every time the old woman moved the little white boy clung heavily to her dress and she sighed at the weight of all the world's burdens and went on counting cherries of love that were lost in the blossoms; and the little white boy sat laughing and grunting his white-foxed delight.

A for Abraham, they taught the little white boy. B for Bethlehem, they told the little white boy. C for Christ, they whispered to the little white boy. 'A –' said the little white boy, very slowly, very sadly, very thoughtfully, and a whole new world hovered in the clouds above him. D for Donkey, muttered the old peasant woman. E for Engine, mumbled the time-trodden farmer. F for Friday, laughed the wobble-chinned farmer's wife, counting her money on the table. 'B –'

repeated the little white boy watching the fields rear up and the hedges sprouting into a hundred tangled thorn-bushes, with raining roses. G for God, snapped the farmer's sister through her prim-toned nose and her frustrated mouth. H for Harry, said the slouching cowboy with his clanging pails, squinting upon a stool. I for Isaac, remarked the vicar's wife and the woman in the sweetshop and the tired postman and the council hedge-trimmer and the publican's family and the uneasy woman in the cottage over the hill. 'C –' murmured the little white boy to himself, rolling a tender tongue. J and K and L and M and N and OPQRSTUVWXY, screamed the intrusive voices of the city factories and the mechanised murmurs of the shining suburbs, and out of the clouds came the steady tapping of a million imported typewriters and the flying sheets of notepaper built the walls of a huge hall and a long street and a winding chain of window shops. Z, murmured a woodland stream so that only the little white boy could hear as he ran away from the buzzing world's sobs.

The little white boy climbed a five-barred gate and danced down a sloping field of buttercups into the friendly shadow of three oak trees. I was born in the buttercups something said inside his marrowed bones and he hitched up his bright grey pants and rolled through the buttercups like a mongrel dog. I am all alone now thought the little white boy happily as he put his foot on the weed-strewn path through the woods. He put one foot on a bramble and another foot on a stone and another foot on a broken tree trunk and another foot splashed in yesterday's pool of water. The path wound away like a snake among the tomato sticks. The little white boy sang as he skipped along the snake-bellied wood path. The path went neither up nor down but straight along and the little white boy bowled along like an effortless snowball. Once upon a time there was a lovely princess and a handsome prince and a wicked baron, sang the little white boy, and the shadows of them flitted in and out of the trees with the crazy morning sunshine. I'll climb a tree thought the little white boy, and he picked one with stubbled branches and clinging vines and his rough red feet crouched up the stern trunk. What a tall tree he thought, as the green soot stung his nostrils and his hair clotted with the gritty leaves. But I'm up he thought, and he stood on the last branch and looked down to see the floating ground. He poked his head from under a shady leaf and dived into the clear sunshine. What a lovely day thought the little white boy, and he leaped from the treetop and over the wood and spread himself over a wide cornfield. A mongrel dog came and licked his hand and a broody hen clucked in the corner haystack. 'Mmmmm ...!' murmured the little white boy. A and B and C chanted the flying rooks but they were blinded by the sun and flew into the stone-wall hedge and crushed their beaks.

From out of the ground winked the large eye of the memoried round woman and the little white boy jumped up in joy and turned a somersault in his solitude. I am the king of the castle he thought, peering behind the cornstalks for the long grey moat. Let's pretend I am a king thought the little white boy, and he stood on a disused plough and cried out to his hundred horses and his bright red followers, and the ants and the worms and the pecking birds saluted him from their Mediterranean groves. The cuckoo howled in the woods and the rooks squawked out of the clouds and a young pony whinnied as it raced round and round its homeland. 'Yah!' snorted the little white boy, and he hurled a small stick into the air as his javelin, and the brown spattered cows eyed him reflectively.

The farm was on a hill and the hill was on a mountain and the mountain lay shimmering in the waters of a lake. The little white boy swam through the lake and climbed the mountain and scrambled up the hill and he stood in the open field. He breathed the lilac sweet air and it tickled his throat and the perfumes drugged his lungs and swelled his bulging stomach with their sweet meals. He knelt on the brown earth and felt the warmth enter his body, smoothing over his skin and tingling his excited bones. He closed his eyes and saw the sun streaming into the orchard and the faces of the plump girls and the singing men were sudden smiles. He cocked one ear and caught the faint sullen tomb-beat of a city omnibus and a bargain-sale basement; he cocked the other ear for the wailing violins of the afternoon breezes; he opened both ears and there was the drowning sweep of all the world's chattering birds strutting along green treetops and surveying the vast snow fields of swaying yellow corn.

The little white boy who could say A and B and C lay with his back on the old green earth and stared up into the newborn sky, watching hidden horsemen riding over the cloudless hills. Out of one wise eye he saw the sun like a great round balloon, and he pricked its fat tummy with a finger. Out of another wise eye he saw the moon like a nodding old man, and he scratched its pointed nose with another finger. One two, button my shoe, sang the little white boy, and he kicked up his heels and stood one foot on the sun's round belly and one foot on the moon's thin beak and tickled their bald pates with his dancing toes. Three four, knock at the door, sang the little white boy, and he folded his tiny fist and beat on the great dome of the sky and heard faraway bells ringing. Five six, pick up sticks, sang the little white boy, but he couldn't be bothered and he couldn't remember any more and he was content to paddle in the blue sea and to sail gold and silver ships, far and away across indigo horizons.

The fruit trees groaned in their sweet birth pangs.
The pickers sang low and softly as they plucked the harvest.
The hens were preening in the Sunday sunshine.
A dog barked carelessly in the dark shade of the house.
A clock ticked, tick tock, tick tock, just a lazy old clock.

The little white boy shut his eyes. Serenely pouted his round red lips as if for a forgotten kiss of some milky white breast. And fell asleep.

2

When you grow up you will be a great man sang the water reeds and the white boy twitched in his sleep. It's time you went to school young fellow said the grumpy farmer, a hundred years ago. The long road over the hills was white and dusty and led into space and the flat buildings that weighed down the grey hairs of a sleeping headmaster, in his nightmares. The black easel and the smelling white chalk throttled the sweet afternoon air and the sunshine was boxed in the square window frames. The floor was wooden and dirty and trodden on a thousand times by ghostly feet, and the row of wood desks were a forest of memories. The ink-stands welled up with old flowing blood and smudged the strewn books.

And when you grow up you will be a great man sang the empty water reeds and grew slowly over the shadow of the lost white boy. A thousand black boys marched past the alter-faced gown and mortar and sang the dirge of another day. A thousand black hands saluted the tilted arithmetic table and the tumbling French nouns struck a jangling bell. A thousand black faces stared out of the fences of wire and coughed uneasily upon the hard cold stones. Through a mirror of water shone the faces and the hands of the thousand black boys and lost in the shimmering gleam was the phosphorescent white boy with the mocking smile.

Hallelula! Hallelula! Hallelula! they sang in the subsidised chapel and the mournful hairs of an ape rustled over the Book of the World. Praise ye the Lord! sang the thousand black boys in a bursting treble. Praise ye the Lord! sang the white boy with a cold tear gleaming down his nose and his creased trousers folded on a dusty floor. Praise ye the Lord! sang the white boy dropping a round penny in his long fingers and pressing it softly against his rubber leg. Praise ye the Lord! sang the white boy with the curled fair hair and he rubbed his nose against the smooth skin of an exercise book and watched a logarithm table climb into the sky. Yea, verily! echoed the thousand black boys in their cold steel cases, and a testing tube flamed in the tired laboratory. Hallelula! they sang in their surging voices and the empty chapel echoed with the discordant strains of a rust-begotten organ ... Hallelula! Hallelula! Hallelula!

I wonder why? thought the white boy sitting at the table with the jam-jarred flesh plates. I have a clean shirt and long trousers and a boil on the side of my head and tonight we shall have buns in the dormitory but I hate the old South Welsh master, I wish he were dead. The white boy's books weighed thirty-nine pounds and he wore them like a pumpkin on his chest. The white boy's pen was stained red and he licked the point with a long furred tongue and spat at the children playing leapfrog. An iron band ran round his head like a fallen crown and he winked a forgotten grimace. In the morning was the beginning, in the afternoon was the middle, and in the evening was the end; and the desks were chalky with dead confetti. He sat on his shining trousers and swam into a Greek memory and he cried out words that belonged to timeless dead men. There were a thousand black boys and fifty sad apes and they breathed the same air in a prison of one hundred and seven days and their sleeping fumes mixed in the fuggy night.

He's a tell-tale chanted the whispering voices. He's a dunce chanted the whispering ghost voices. He's a thief and a dog and a sneak and a copycat and a greedy pig and he has to do two thousand lines for a hairy ape because he climbed a forbidden steeple chanted the rising, falling, whispering ghost voices. He's this and he's that and he's all these, too, grunted the apes of the artificial halls, scratching their steady pens on the rough paper.

The white boy walked fifteen times round a square yard and recognized the grey stone schoolhouse. Once he climbed the ironwire fence, tearing blue flesh into bone, and stumbled into a greasy lane and listened to a trotting baker's cart while he shuddered from the grim grey happiness and thought he smelt the fields in spring. Come back, come back, come back at once! yelled a hagless tooth from her washing on her private lawn; and she waved a wandering finger. The white boy made his long white face and ground his steely-point eyes into hate and threw a hoarse laugh against the safe fence. He followed the lane round the grey prison and away up the hill until his head lay rolling in a weary gutter and he heard the stamping feet of an old bearded man, and he slid back into the undergrowth.

The twenty white beds that lay in a row were his field of corn, and they swam in a pool of heavy incense. Twenty candles flickered in the early twilight and he lay and heard the music of rustling clothes. Now I am a white boy, he thought, as he washed away the soap with the cool free water. Now I am a warm white boy, he thought, as he rubbed the towel slowly up and down his sullen limbs. There were twenty black boys but he was a warm white boy, he thought, looking vaguely into the blackness of the mirror. He saw the beauty of a dark-haired boy with an Indian skin and a beckoning finger. He followed the strength of a square-faced wrestler from the antique world. He worshipped the soft skin of the fair-faced son with the laughing mouth ... Never had man such beauty cried the dark-haired boy. Nor such strength spat the square-faced wrestler. Nor such a soft soft skin whispered the fair-faced son. They wrapped slow hands about the white boy and entwined his tongue of kindled flame and the white coverlets were melting into soft oblivion. I must not, wrote the white boy on a mystic waxboard, and his mind filled with a hundred lines and he started like a jellyfish and screamed into three empty faces. I must not, I must not, I must not, I must not, I must not screamed the white boy, white-faced. I must not, I must not, I must not, I must not panted the white boy, puffing fear into a horizon. Thou shalt not! read the tenth morning prefect in the tired chapel, and the white boy fled with his gathering limbs and trembled on a hard wood floor under the dawn. I am I learnt the white boy in his never-forgetting old mind.

The bells of the morning had no blood-warmed veins for their song, the invitation to the bitten pen-end was rung in cold wet ink and the slippery tiles outside were beaten with winterness. The white boy clung to his own white bed and shrank from the curling looks of twenty black-faced boys, then he fled into the bleak book rooms. The white boy wrapped himself in a hundred pages from a hundred books and drank a Hamlet wine and ate an Endymion sausage until he was sick on the best stone parquet. I am the writer of a hundred pages, he thought, and his iron clad pen flew into the wilderness. I am the adder of a hundred sums, he thought, and his mind turned a clicking somersault. I am the speaker of a hundred languages he thought, and he picked words out of an inked French Prose and threw them carelessly into the wayward air. I am the learner of everything thought the white boy (he's a dunce, he's a sneak, he's a thief, murmured the blown voices) and his pound-weight books crashed around him like a tank-spewn wall of an old arcade. His cold legs stamped into the far night and shone in the dying candlelight, and his head rolled over the sullen desks. His long fingers crushed a pebble of paper on a pierced pencil point and the lines of the words were curling worms on a piano's black keys. I am the learner, I must be the learner, I am the learner of everything repeated the white weary boy with the falling curly locks and the frightened memory. I am the great learner boasted the white boy. He sat on a stony planet, swinging circles far from the green fields, and his drowsy body was a machine in a world of smoke. He decimated the atom into a wilderness of doubt and crouched with his horned head in his hands and a labouring verb twisting into his small round greyness. He opened a book at the first page and the sudden gusts blew into his downcrested face all the other thousand unending pages, and he felt cold and heavy.

One hundred and seven more days said the white boy. One hundred and six more days said his friend with the squint. They walked slowly down the drive and slowly up the drive and slowly down the drive and slowly up the drive.

One hundred and five more days said the white boy. One hundred and four more days said his friend with the squint. They ran round a football field with a chariot of fire, the heat tore the ground and burnt their feet and they cooled in the spraying aftermath.

One hundred and three more days said the white boy. One hundred and two more days said his friend with the squint. They read a Sunday newspaper about a war and a meeting and a floating body in a duckpond and the woman called Mrs Josephine Johnson (31) and the suave lawyer with the hotel-room ticket.

One hundred and one more days said the white boy. One hundred more days said his friend with the squint. They sat in the greased saloon with the dying fish and potatoes and furtively read an old magazine while the school apes paced past, and they glanced owlishly at the jowled paper man and the rough red face of the waiter.

Ninety-nine more days said the white boy at his lonely desk and his half-open books. 'Pay attention!' intoned the whine of the two-legged wizards. 'Pay attention!' muttered the sleeping beard beard of the old headmaster, nodding wisely.

Ninety-nine, ninety-eight, ninety-seven, ninety-six, ninety-five-four-three-two-one! shouted the white boy stubbornly. Ninety-eight! called his squint-eyed friend from a gloomy wall, and a huge cloud hung over his shoulder. Ninety-nine!

repeated the white boy stubbornly and opened his mouth wide
to read all his candle-burnt knowledge. But a hand gripped his
heart and squeezed his veins and tortured his bowels, and jelly
flowed into his rubber legs and the vast trees suddenly
shuddered.

The white boy looked up and saw a shadow girl flit over his
open window. The white boy's eyes were pencils that traced the
soft waves of the rippling shadow girl, were swords that pierced
the flowing robes and sank into the unexpected flesh. 'Oh ...'
said the white boy with the wide open mouth and the round
round eyes and he lay in the wondering dusk with his scattered
books falling into an unheeded pit and from somewhere came
a howling and a shrieking, and from out of the old clouds of
time fled the tearing winds, blowing him helplessly over the
horizon and far away.

3

Ah, but only young once but only young once but only young
once, said the wind in the trees, said the kindly breeze, and the
fiery years paused.

The boy and the girl held soft hands together and walked
unafraid down the long-treed lanes, in the twilight promise of
a summer.

They climbed the winding lane and the old-cut mountain
path, and they wandered through the night groves and the
pleasant smells of the high old heavens. The boy and the girl
crossed the bare peat carpets and ran up ten stony staircases,
while the odd lights of the village flickered helplessly in the
abyss. The boy and the girl swam through the rustling lake
waters in the benevolent nakedness of the moon, their white
limbs tingling with tears. The boy and the girl stretched their
dripping elf-forms on to the cold rock bankside and shivered
in their apprehensive caresses, like the stone and the water.

I am the white boy and this is the white girl thought the boy
wonderingly, sure from his mind-raced smiles in the fields and
his twenty bed dreams. I am the white boy and this is the white
girl thought the little white boy and the white boy and the boy
of the sentimental diary. Three witches howled on their

haunches in a cavern, a thousand black boys danced on in their seaside towns.

This is the white girl, this quiver of a loving hair in my own pulsed heart thought the boy. He looked slowly at the grave face and smiled a life into the drowned eyes, he laid a hand on the breasts and they were round red petals. This is the shadow girl of my long young life whispered the boy while a thousand shadows shook their rolling laughter in the mountain mists.

They climbed to the pinnacle, the rock-strewn, dust-made pinnacle of a life and a mountain. They stood on the high plateau and the whistle-wind blew away the white-robed shyness of the fresh girl and the smoke-stained fingers of the boy were pure with sudden whiteness. The white-wind blew around the fanned flames of the two-leaded twigs with an angry howl. The boy stood strong and sure on his iron rock and held out his long white hands. Come to me, come to me, my shadow girl he said gravely.

The boy held out his loving hands to the blossom girl. The boy touched the white-stone shoulders and felt them melting into cream, and the whistle-wind blew the spots in an angry hail into his eyes. The boy's living hand circled the drooping breasts and felt them stiffen into two iron daggers that pierced the long blue veins of his yearned fingers. The boy pressed his manhood against the quivered shimmer of the golden girl and felt the dust blow up between them like a great stone wall of an ancient castle. The boy kissed the full red lips of the stone girl and tasted the wet thickness of blood, filling his mouth with paste-death.

O, love! cried out the boy, with the fearful throb in his head. O, love! echoed the rollicking mountains, shaking their bellies. O, love! mocked the three sleeping witches in their shrewish hide-out! My love went away, went away, da-di-da-da-di-da, hummed the haunted saxophones of a thousand dancing black boys, assembling grin-eyed on the mountain top. The boy screamed and hurled his arms around the girl, the blue-eyed girl, the shadow girl, he felt the melting cream and the steel daggers and the walls and the bloods, he crushed them to him in the desperate vapour of air. A shadow girl danced from him into the leering dusk and poised on the edge of the mountain and blew him a rose-blood kiss that darkened the air, and tumbled headlong on to the jagged rocks of a thousand twinkling villages and the clouds rained tears.

But the clock ticked and the sun rose and the sun fell and the moon was cold so cold, like an old cold stone, and gone away was the little white boy and gone away was the white boy. Now there was only the boy with the greying cheeks and the yesterday's smile.

It's a big world and a cashandcarry world, thought the boy, and so he worshipped the jingling coins, putting them against his lips and breathing on them until their warmth made his blood race. And so he filled them into his bulging pockets until the weight pinned him to the ground, while the coins rusted away.

It's a hard world and a class-unconscious world, thought the boy, and so he wore a coloured bow and a bright red shirt and memorised his careful slogans, the Liberty, the Equality, the Fraternity. And so he platform-postulated and signed a thousand peasant petitions and shouted a million metaphors and died a hundred dream deaths for causes, while the world went to war.

It's a sin world and a ghostwithoutholy world, thought the boy, and so he found God at afternoon tea-parties and took him home to keep on a chain in a portable kennel. And so he devoured rows of little black books in hasty meals and worshipped the gown of an Eastern mystery, while his neighbour starved.

It's a bore world and a glitterbrass world, thought the boy, and so he grew long hair and saw through the haze of imported cigars and slobbered down long streams of hot gold gin. And so he lived for the wooden harlot and the black-faced trumpeter and the pipe of forgetfulness, while the golden years cried.

Outside the dark streets of the city gleam in the moonshine, the silent roofs crumble in loneliness, the old monuments fade like every season's flowers. Down the long roadways walks humanity and up the long roadways walks humanity, and there is everything old before and everything new behind. At every corner some travellers turn this way and some travellers turn that way, and perhaps they find happiness and perhaps they just vanish into the dust, and all the time the silly old clock goes tick-tock, tick-tock, just a silly old clock ... Oh, lay your tired haunches in some ordinary bed and raise some pleasant family and weed your Sunday morning garden, it's simpler that way.

Ah well, thought the boy, and he arose and went out into the roadway.

Ah well, thought the boy, and he took a long deep breath of fresh air.

Ah well, thought the boy, and he opened his eyes wide at the sun.

The boy sighed in the early morning glory. *There's always the dew and the green green grass and to-morrow and to-morrow and to-morrow.* And walked on into the exciting years.

XVII

Special Edition

On the day of the special edition Cole got up an hour earlier than usual. Otherwise he knew the thing would overwhelm him like a giant, runaway snowball. It had happened to him on a previous occasion. He had been trying frantically to retain his mental grip upon a thousand and one worrying tasks – suddenly everything broke loose. His head began swimming; a sensation of tightness fastened around his throat; for some moments he found it impossible to speak. He started trembling all over, and the next thing he was crumpled into the chair, crying and weeping like a child instead of the cynical news-editor of a busy provincial newspaper. Someone fetched a doctor, and eventually he was taken home in a taxi. As a result the paper appeared two hours late, everyone had to work overtime, several important news stories were overlooked. It had taken him a week to summon up the courage to return and face the thin-lipped comments of Rankin, the fussy, dapper editor – the sarcastic sympathy of Stack, the chief sub-editor. It was not so much that he feared them as that he hated their superior attitude, resented their being presented with one more opportunity to make him feel humiliated. He had never been able to forget it even to this day; the remembrance was always there, along with a hundred other sores, rankling and festering. Just like the sores and pains tucked deep in his chest, the constant pricking of restless ulcers that lay, like time-bombs, under the white rotundity of his middle-aged paunch. Every movement, somehow, seemed to bring its twitch of pain, its signal of discomfort, its niggling reminder of the steady advancement of age and ill-health. He was fifty-one, a small disappointed man, clinging doggedly to dislikes and envies, and never more so than on this long-dreaded day of worry, as he climbed unwillingly out of the bed's warmth and started dressing, shivering at the touch of the dark March morning.

He left his wife still asleep, her fat, rather sweaty face relaxed and gaping, familiar lines criss-crossing her forehead, ageing her mouth and eyes. Usually she got up first and had his unvarying, diet-prescribed breakfast of dry toast and milk ready for him when he came down. She was good to him, a faithful servant to the whims and caprices of his recurrent ill-health ... Let her sleep on, now. His reasoning was born neither of love nor pity, merely out of a sort of weary acceptance of their twenty-six years of married life. He went down and into the labour-saving kitchen of their home on one of the Corporation's housing estates. Vaguely going through the process of making breakfast, he burnt the porridge and over-heated the milk, which he was only allowed to drink luke-warm. He could not be bothered to make toast and ate, instead, some thin water-biscuits. The pieces crunched uneasily between a neat row of white upper dentures and the straggly, yellow-tipped lowers that were still his own. He swallowed awkwardly and without pleasure, the while he stared distastefully at a pile of greasy plates, relics of the previous night's meal. Waiting for the milk to cool he was suddenly interrupted by a sharp jab of irritation in his lower abdomen. Christ, oh Christ, he thought, a good start to the day. Giving up hope of the milk, he arose and, stooping to avoid further disturbance of his stomach, went to put on his thickest overcoat. Winding a pale scarf round his neck he studied himself in the hall mirror. He saw a coarsened, rather haggard face, drooping flat cheeks, a small and petulant mouth, a wide, rather yellowy forehead, deep-set and over-darkened eyes; his head, narrow and elongated, showed inescapable traces of oncoming baldness under the streaky grey of his hair. Frowning, he put on an old trilby hat and pulled the brim low over his eyes. Turning up the coat collar, he hunched his shoulders and plunged his hands deep into the pockets. There ... that looked a bit neater, more purposeful. As long as those threatening signs of weakness – the bald spots, the thin chest, the varicose legs – as long as they remained out of sight they could be thrust out of mind. For a time, anyway. He gave a twist to his hat. Well, he was a man of responsibilities, when all was said and done – a man in control, an essential pivot, a key to a system. And today the responsibility was very special. At the thought he could almost feel the heavy weights beginning to fall upon the narrow hump of his shoulders.

He stepped to the foot of the stairs and called out: 'Goodbye, dear. Back late tonight. Bye!' Then, hunching up moodily, he went out into the familiar morning scene, the long lines of neat, grey stone houses, and began walking down towards the centre of the town.

It was a town that belonged, comfortably and decisively, to the heart of the English Midlands. It was a town built out of staunch labour and enterprise, paid for with good, hard, well-earned cash, fortunate in the services of numerous loyal and high-minded citizens and in the solid possession of a variety of useful if rather uninspiring institutions and developments … a sombre but impressive town hall, a grey, scholarly library, a bright red brick omnibus station, a series of well-kept parks and playing fields, a number of modern schools and ambitious blocks of offices, some highly productive engineering and light industrial plants and factories … all settled under a gentle, hazy umbrella of sooty smoke and surrounded by a broad new circular roadway which enabled unappreciative travellers fastidiously to pass all further acquaintance with the town.

It was along part of this by-pass that Cole lived, but it took him less than twenty minutes to walk into the centre, to the town hall square in one corner of which, a streak of welcome brightness in the subdued surroundings, stood the recently rebuilt offices of the *Utherton Evening Post*. The offices were tall and clean-lined, fused into a majestic six-storey edifice, dotted with extra wide sliding-glass windows that let in the maximum amount of light (and, as some found, cold). At the top of the building was a flat roof-garden where employees could if they so wished, and should the variable Midlands climate permit, spend their off-periods in sunbathing. These and many other pleasant advantages of the abode of one of Utherton's leading civic institutions had been glowingly described at the time of the official opening by the Mayor, after the building had been enlarged and redecorated in celebration of the acquisition of the newspaper by a remote London syndicate. On that occasion everything had been gleaming with newness – new paint, new furniture, new printing presses, new delivery vans – also faces, most of the old staff having been sacked and replaced, largely by strangers from London. Cole, who had then been one of the lucky ones, had lived ever since on what he felt to be the edge of a permanently bubbling volcano ... liable to rise to dangerous heights at a badly missed story, even at some internal mismanagement. Certain to erupt disastrously at the slightest flaw in the production of a special edition.

Feeling the thin, nervous tingle of the day's tension gripping his body, Cole walked swiftly through the swing-doors, across the marble-tiled hall and up to the long reporters' room on the first floor. As he came among the tall, over-bearing walls of the corridors, the glass door-partitions glittering from hidden electric lights, he felt the bright, dusty inside world encompassing him. Entering the reporters' room, as yet deserted, his eyes saw the rows of paper-strewn desks like some great, awaiting battle arena – squat, shiny typewriters like brooding tanks. And battle it was, he thought sourly, leaning over his desk in the corner and staring out of the window across the square to where he could just see one grey corner of the offices of the *Utherton Evening News*, locally owned and steadily maintaining its popularity – greatest menace of all to the day's security. Supposing things went wrong, the *News* had a great, unforgivable 'beat' in getting out their special edition of the day's oncoming big story? Supposing all the careful preparations were wasted? Cole, felt the nervousness reach down into his bowels. So much to do, time wasting, already half-past eight ... His harboured uneasiness boiled up resentfully. Where was everyone? Didn't they realise the difficulties involved in getting out a special edition? He thought morosely: they don't care, they have no sense of duty, they'd be glad if I lost my job ... He began pacing up and down the room. When they started trickling in, half an hour later, he was already in one of his worst tempers.

The first was Atkinson, a youngster, no more than nineteen, the son of some friend of Rankin's who had expressed a desire to be a journalist and had to be humoured because of Rankin's officious backing.

'What time do you call this?' snapped Cole. 'Do you think special editions can be brought out just like that –?' He snapped his fingers together.

Atkinson's fresh, eager face flushed up.

'I'm very sorry, sir.'

Cole thought of his own youth, long laborious years as a badly paid junior reporter on remote provincial weeklies, doing the work of two or three men, wearing himself to the bone – then being turned out to make way for a friend of the proprietor's, or a less expensive premium pupil. Now these young whipper-snappers came along, like Atkinson. Why shouldn't they suffer?

He glared across at Atkinson, eyeing with distaste the baby face, the curling lock of hair, check-coloured shirt, the green sporty tie.

'Well, get on with it ... get out and make the calls. Go on now ...' He could not resist a sneer. 'Perhaps you wouldn't mind leaving your leisurely read of the morning papers till a bit later?'

Atkinson went out, colouring. Ah, I know their tricks, thought Cole. Feeling a bit more pleased as he looked round and saw that Stack had come in the far corner of the room; a stout bespectacled, cheerful old man whom the rest of the office looked upon as a sort of benevolent father. Cole flustered and began rummaging among his papers. Action. Get things under way. Get on with it. He picked up his schedule, and jumped to his feet and went over to where Stack was standing.

'This special edition,' he said with heavy worriedness. 'Christ, I hope everything goes all right ... I was up till about one this morning trying to work out this schedule.' He thrust the paper challengingly before Stack. There, make something of that, get to work, you fat smiling frog, he thought.

'Were you really?' said Stack. He eyed Cole sardonically. 'You worry too much, old man.' He handed the schedule back. 'In any case, no use giving me this. It's up to you to provide the material, we'll see it gets down to the machines as soon as possible.' He nodded and went out and across to the sub-editors' room.

Cole breathed heavily, a whisly breath. Swine, swine, swine! Always putting the burden on me, you don't care, I have to worry ... He muttered to himself ... without him the whole thing would collapse like a pack of cards. They never thought of that. He felt the stab of pain back in his stomach, and limped back to his corner.

In a queer sort of way he was rather fond of that corner. It was partly cut off from the rest of the room by a glass partition; there was something solid and authoritative about it, it was some sort of a concrete symbol of his advancement, such as it was. He liked to sit back and look at the two telephones, the piles of papers and books, the neat signboard stating, in faded gold letters: BERNARD COLE, News Editor. Sometimes he would sit for long periods, half dreaming, perhaps reflecting: I can lift that receiver and get Rawlinson, one of the district men outside Utherton, and order him to go and cover the Farnton Agricultural Show. Or I can get Bromley, the other outside man, and send him on some equally tiring and unwelcome mission. Often, just for the devil of it, he did exactly that. Another thing he liked to do was to call round the edge of the partition, round about five o'clock in the evening, when everybody was looking forward to going home, and apportion some unimportant evening assignment to one of the younger reporters. He enjoyed watching them approach, apprehension transfixing their faces, a faint spark of hope in their eyes. These were his few moments of apparent joviality. 'I'm sure you'll do an excellent account of the Utherton Temperance Society's Annual Concert, Groves,' he might say. And in the morning if Groves had conscientiously written half a column he would brusquely order it to be cut to five lines ... Other times he lectured them on the appalling quality of their style, speaking in his loudest voice so that they would be mortified to think of the whole office hearing their discomfiture. The only time Cole didn't enjoy being in his corner was when he was penned in there by the unexpected arrival of Rankin – plump, well-set, stupid, fussy, bothering, Rankin – but, nevertheless, Rankin the boss.

Orpington, the librarian, a lean, stooping aesthetic individual, came over with a sheaf of photographs in his hand. He leant over and placed them in front of Cole. They were pictures of members of a dramatic society in various poses.

'I understand we're running a feature on The Drama in Utherton – sometime next week –' he began.

Cole spat into the wastepaper basket.

'Christ!' He exclaimed. 'A next-week feature – you come and talk to me about that now – there's a whole bloody special edition to occupy today – or hadn't you realised?'

He watched, with pleasure, Orpington's prim face screwing up with distaste. He always tried to use unpleasant words in front of this prim prig.

'What are you doing about it, anyway?' demanded.

Orpington tried to look haughty.

'Arrangements have been made for full photographic coverage. Both Armfield and Simpkins have gone off. I can't do more than that.'

He turned and walked off stiffly. It was obvious that his leisurely peace had been upset. Cole felt satisfied. He leant back in his chair a bit more comfortably. Show the buggers how, he thought.

The phone rang. Idly he answered. A sharp voice demanded:

'Come to my office at once, please.'

It was Rankin.

Normally it was about eleven o'clock in the morning before Rankin put in a leisurely appearance in time to do his correspondence, issue one or two pinpricking notes to various members of his staff and pass a generally pleasant hour before making fussy preparations for one of his inevitable luncheon appointments. As editor of one of Utherton's leading newspapers he occupied most of his time in entertaining and being entertained by suitably important citizens of the town, particularly influential councillors, well-placed members of local society, and the most substantial of Utherton's business heads and retail traders – a form of occupation which at least had an encouraging effect on advertisement revenue, even if it contributed surprisingly little to the editorial news column. This morning, however, he was already settled in the deep swing-chair behind his huge mahogany desk, a slightly ruffled air faintly disturbing his otherwise smooth and polished façade of ease and aplomb.

'Ah, there you are at last, Cole,' he said fussily. He began rummaging vaguely amongst little heaps of documents piled neatly about his desk. 'I take it you've remembered about the special edition today?' Without waiting for an answer, he went on: 'Big job, you know, very important that things should go without a hitch … Thought I'd better be on the spot to see things are – ahem – ticking over, you know. Don't want any mistakes, do we?' He smiled with false benevolence in Cole's direction. Somehow, by the introduction of the delicate plural prefix he had managed already to establish for himself a vague, pleasant sense of authority in the day's event, while quite clearly leaving all the responsibility to Cole.

'Now,' said Rankin, rubbing two podgy, well-kept hands together. 'What are we doing about it, eh?'

He listened, now and then interjecting a doubtful grunt, while Cole uneasily ran through his exhaustive and complex schedule of action, detail by detail. Cole knew that it was doubtful if Rankin understood more than about a half of what he was saying. All the same the knowledge could not save him from twisting awkwardly from one foot to another as he spoke, and feeling the excruciating sensation of fear in his bowels – a sensation he could trace right back to days when he was awaiting his master's examination of school homework.

'Quite, quite,' said Rankin after a time, leaning back and eyeing his fingers contemplatively. He had a curious, petty mind that automatically thought out unimportant, nibbling side-issues. He eyed Cole reprovingly. 'Of course I realise this is rather a big job to handle … Nevertheless, I hope you won't overlook certain essential details.' He paused gravely. 'For instance – I see you've omitted to arrange to have a liaison messenger boy from my office to yours, eh?'

'Yes. I'm sorry, I'll see to it,' said Cole in an undertone, restraining himself with a great effort from pointing out that it would be quite simple for Rankin to come down to the reporters' room.

'Well, well,' said Rankin forgivingly, 'we can only do our best.' He got up and strolled easily over to the wide windows, hung with heavy rust tapestries. He fitted like a neat jig-saw piece into the pattern of comfortable success. In his presence Cole felt like a piece of dirt upon the carpet.

Rankin looked at his wrist-watch.

'Now I've got an appointment.' He cast an ambiguous, half sympathetic, half threatening glance at Cole. 'We'll see things through, eh? Mmm ... Yes.' Grunting a trifle sardonically, he began putting his things together ready to go out: a bulky imposing brief-case, an impressive sheaf of documents, a wad of typewritten memorandums. He carried them about with him wherever he went. Only a few, like Cole, knew these were part of the façade; and they didn't matter. In fact Cole would gladly give up all his thirty odd years of genuine, hard-earned experience – much good it had done him, anyway – for the privilege of wearing Rankin's shoes. Comfort – confidence – leisure – no worrying. To be able to whisk in and out of the gigantic cream-coloured building as if it were no more tying or important that a clubhouse ... Instead of being hammered and screwed in a cast-iron position like any cog in the printing presses below. Cole thought morosely, as he padded dutifully along unending internal corridors. Passing a clock he saw it was already ten o'clock. He began running, frightened at the possibilities of his prolonged inactivity.

Back at his desk, picking nervously with a matchstick between the cracks of his teeth, he mentally rehearsed, for about the twentieth time, his arrangements for covering the big story. Waring was to phone through the main comprehensive story. Dickinson would do a special descriptive report. Orwell and Sharpe would try and get some personality angles. (Had they got there yet? Would they miss something the *News'* men would get?). Then there were the telephone arrangements (Had the lines been booked with the Post Office? Were the office telephones in order? Would there be enough telephonist-receivers to go round?). And typewriters (supposing there weren't enough? Or they were all wrong, went out of order?). And pictures. And captions. And times for last copy. And times for the last fudge items. (Could he trust Orpington? Would Stack co-operate? Were the machine-men downstairs reliable? Had the transport manager got the speediest possible system for the vans?). Again and again the thoughts circled around his mind, the process interrupted every now and then by an odd vision – with a curious mixture of fear and fellow-sympathy – of Morrison, his opposite number of the *News*, going through the same complex procedure. Morrison was younger, tougher, more determined. Supposing he fixed things so that the *News* got their edition out first? Cole felt a tiny, mute sound fill his throat, a still-born groan. It would be unthinkable, disastrous; the world of security he had so precariously built around him would come tumbling down. There would be inquests, accusations, savage condemnations; they would all come back to him, his the unbearable, yet unget-riddable responsibility; finally there would be wires buzzing to London, peremptory orders, shufflings and re-arrangements: dismissal. At the last thought Cole found himself thinking, oddly, jealously, of his wife. By now she would be up and pottering about the house; at least she had nothing to bother about except lunch. While he – he sat there, alone and forsaken, on the brink of disaster … Alone? The sweat dampened his yellow forehead. No, it mustn't be, he must get help. He looked wildly across the office, noting the empty desks of the men who had departed on the big story. Hell, there was hardly anyone left. 'Atkinson!' he called urgently … damn, he'd be out an hour yet. 'Groves!' Cursing, he remembered that Groves had been assigned to the petty sessions.

With a great effort he controlled his spinning brain, reached out for the telephone.

'Get Rawlinson!' he snapped at the operator. 'And after that, get Bromley.'

A few minutes later he was, not without a feeling of satisfaction, ordering Rawlinson to catch the next bus into Utherton. He knew that for several weeks past the district man had been carefully planning to take this week-end off.

Then Bromley, who complained plaintively that he hadn't had a Saturday afternoon off for three months, and that he had a brother-in-law specially coming over to see him that afternoon, on Army leave.

Cole mouthed into the telephone, his eyes bright with anger:

'I can't help your private affairs, the only thing I'm concerned with is this special edition. We must get it out on time … You'll have to put your relative off … Be here as soon as you can.'

He leant back, thinking that's two men to hand, anyway, wondering if he dared feel a little less frightened. No, here was trouble coming. He watched, mesmerised, the approach of a cherubic, tousled-haired 'copy' boy. It was a careless, swaggering approach, it was obvious that the boy hadn't a care in the world. He was whistling inharmoniously.

'For God's sake stop whistling!' exclaimed Cole irritably. He snatched a proffered piece of paper from the boy's hand. It was a message from the subs' room. Could they please have, *within half-an-hour* a story for the early ordinary edition – enough to fill two columns, a preliminary introduction to the day's big story.

Cole crumpled the piece of paper. Swines, why didn't they let him know before? It wasn't shown on his schedule. What did they think he was, a magician? He looked round the room sourly. There was only Johnson, grey head bent behind a mound of books in one corner – the eldest and most experienced reporter, used to pursuing a leisurely routine, providing every day a useful, meaty story which had been obtained in comfort and at his own time, probably sitting over a cup of tea in someone's office. Usually Cole was a little nervous of assaulting the other's tranquillity. Now he thought, why shouldn't he suffer as well? – and went over to the desk and brusquely demanded a two-column story, at once.

Waiting with ill-controlled impatience for Johnson's story, Cole turned to the morning papers, flicking his eyes over the headlines in the vague hope of finding an item which might suit. It had all happened before. He ran through a column of military awards. Not one of the recipients came from Utherton. The nearest came from Liverpool. Perhaps it would be worth a paragraph? Then he remembered the day ... the paper would be chock full with the big story, pictures and everything. Nothing else mattered.

At mid-day he passed through Groves' police court report, a special item from London, and Johnson's pedantically efficient story. A sudden weariness led him to forgo his usual pleasure of finding fault with each item, calling the writer before him and sarcastically pulling it to bits. The tempo was swelling too rapidly for bothering with things like that. Already the great presses below him were running off the early first edition, the race was on ... Already Rankin had been on the phone: 'I trust everything is well ahead, Cole? Mind, I'm relying upon you. I shall be back as soon as I can this afternoon.' (Now you can go off and enjoy your carefree lunch, hated Cole, but silently.) Filled with the desire to pass on his irritation he looked across at Atkinson's blond, bent head.

'Here, you,' he said gruffly, 'You'd better stand by until I come back, in case there are any messages.'

'I don't know how long I shall be,' he added with deliberate vagueness, and went off to have his lunch in the canteen – there to sit sullenly in a corner watching the laughing, chattering crowd of overalled machine-men, girl packers, compositors, advertisement reps, subs and clerks – frowning at them and wondering resentfully why they didn't feel tense and strung up, weary and sick, about this bloody special – and all the time nibbling sourly at his restricted meal of cheese sandwich and a glass of milk.

At two o'clock the first call from Waring came through, just after Cole had returned. Atkinson, who had stood mournfully at the window watching the departure of bus after bus that should have taken him home to a waiting lunch, was about to dart through the door on his thankful way out.

'Hi! – Atkinson, you'll have to take this,' snapped Cole. He swept aside the mute objections. 'Have your lunch later.' He pushed a pale-faced Atkinson into one of the glass telephone booths, fastened a pair of receivers on his head, pointed to the typewriter and shouted: 'There, get on with it!'

He began pacing up and down just behind Atkinson. Could he trust him? Would he get it down correctly? He swung round to where Rawlinson and Bromley were sitting idly.

'Oh, come on ...' They looked puzzled. He hesitated. 'Get into the next booths, ready to relieve.'

He went back to his corner.

'Boy!'

The swaggering one appeared.

'Stand by Atkinson and as soon as he's finished one folio bring it over to me, see?'

'Yessir.' He wished the boy would look flustered or something, instead of calmly squatting by the booth.

He waited tensely, sometimes catching an echo of Waring's sharp, high-pitched voice. 'For Christ's sake!' he muttered to himself. At last he found the inaction unbearable and ran over to the booth.

'What's happening? Why isn't the stuff coming through quicker? Get a move on!'

Atkinson finished the first slip. The boy picked it out of the machine. With a grunt, Cole snatched it and hurried back to his corner. He pored over it. Not so hot, he thought mechanically. I'd have handled it better. He began crossing out a word here, a word there, then suddenly gave it up, fearful of lost time.

'Boy!' he called anxiously. 'Take this to Mr Stack at once.'

As he watched the boy disappearing with irritating leisureliness, his own phone rang. It was Rankin.

'Yes, Mr Rankin?' he said wearily.

'Cole, I've been thinking. I think we ought to make a really special effort and give this story as fully as we possibly can …'

He envisaged Rankin sitting comfortably in the lounge of the Majestic Hotel, where a waiter would bring the telephone to his side.

'I've allocated four thousand words,' he began.

'Nevertheless, Mr Cole –' Rankin's voice took on an unpleasant, determined rasp. 'I think we ought to have, say, a further one thousand words, so that we do the story full justice. Eh?'

'Yes, yes,' said Cole, in the nearest approach to brusqueness he dared use with Rankin. 'Boy!' he called, 'Go and tell Mr Stack we shall be doing an extra one thousand words …' He leant across the desk and shouted to Rawlinson to tell Waring of the pleasant little addition to his afternoon's work.

A plaintive voice dragged him back to the telephone.

'And Cole –'

'Yes, Mr Rankin?'

'I hope you've arranged for that messenger? I shall be back – er – directly.'

'Yes,' he said. Boys, where were the boys? He replaced the receiver and then rang through to the front office. 'Send me a boy at once.' He banged down the receiver irately. Action. No quibbling.

The copy boy re-appeared, looking excited.

'Mr Stack sends his compliments, sir, and says you can't possibly have another thousand words.'

Cole fumed.

'But it's Mr Rankin's orders. Tell him that – oh, never mind!' He stormed across the room and out to the subs' room.

'Mr Stack,' he said, with controlled trembling politeness, 'these are Mr Rankin's orders.'

Stack eyed him with passive benevolence.

'I don't care if they're God Almighty's orders – you can't get a quart into a pint bottle.' He consulted a chart. 'I can just manage another five hundred words.'

Blast you, you'd like to see it late and all the blame on me, thought Cole wildly. Back in the reporters' room he found the other tyepwriters pounding, Groves taking down Dickinson, Rawlinson taking down Orwell, a rather nervous Bromley coping with Sharpe.

Under their feet the huge machines were beating out the birth of the second and last ordinary edition. Cole heard time slipping away from him, with the rumbles of the presses ... He must get on with it, keep everyone up to scratch. He bundled several pages of copy through to the subs; rang up the printing foreman; rang up the transport manager; rang up the packing department. They all sounded to him unconcerned, unaware of the strain upon him.

A moment later the operator from downstairs rang through to say there was a lady waiting with an item of news.

'News? It can't be anything important.' Nothing was important in the world except the one story. 'We're terribly busy ...' But he hesitated, remembering the disastrous results of a previous occasion when he had ignored another caller. He roved his eyes desperately round the room: Johnson, tucked away in a corner, was reading a paper.

'Johnson, into the front office. Someone with a news item.'

Looking on the verge of revolt, Johnson made a heavy, disgruntled departure. As he went out a small, frightened-looking boy entered.

'Who are you, what do you want?' said Cole fiercely. Then he remembered. 'Oh, the messenger boy. Sit here awhile.'

He looked over at the booths. He was sure they were taking it down haphazardly, unthinkingly. He pored over the slips of paper that came before him. Mistakes, mis-spelling, bad grammar. Can't rely on anyone he thought bitterly. He picked up one sheet and went and thrust it in front of Rawlinson.

'I can't make sense of it, ask him what it means.'

Startled, Rawlinson dropped the receivers, picked them up

again and began an involved conversation with an irate Orwell. 'For Lord's sake, don't hold me up, I don't want to be here all night,' came Orwell's plaintive voice. Cole bent down and shouted viciously into the mouthpiece: 'Call yourself a newspaperman!' He stalked away.

His telephone rang again.

'Cole?'

Rankin again.

'Yes, Mr Rankin,' he said in a sort of mechanical drone.

A strange boy, a third boy, appeared laden with the afternoon's post, with agency messages from London, taken over the teleprinter machine. Cole began looking through them, the while Rankin's soft sleepy voice flowed on. '... Held up for a while over an important talk with the Town Clerk ... trust you are doing your best ... relying on you, we must pull together ... I shall be in shortly, have a complete set of galley proofs ready ...' Cole studied the agency messages. He glared at them hopelessly. They'd never get in. Savagely he slashed them down to a few lines each.

'Yes, as you say, Mr Rankin,' he concluded, thankfully.

Over at the booth Atkinson looked distraught.

'What's wrong now?' hurled Cole frantically.

Atkinson stammered.

'I – we've been cut off.' Together they struggled over the telephone, Cole snapping demands to the operator, Atkinson asking every now and then, like a prayer, Hullo? Hullo? Hullo? At last after four minutes' delay, Waring came through. He sounded sour and tired. Sweating profusely, Cole went away ... everything went wrong, these young fools, couldn't trust them ...

Outside he heard the vans roaring off with their copies of the last ordinary issue. In a few minutes they would be back and waiting thought Cole nervously. 'For Christ's sake tell them to get a move on!' he shouted across the room, to no one in particular. The cherub-faced copy boy nodded agreeably.

Cole feverishly studied his time-charts. His phone rang. Stack said: 'Time's getting short, we're waiting on your copy.' Cole struggled with the figures ... four-thirty, four-thirty-five, about ten minutes more. He looked round at the folio numbers on the sheets; surely they were behind?

Looking round he saw Johnson gesticulating at the doorway. He cocked an ear.

'It's a suicide,' said Johnson laconically. 'Prominent member of Utherton Corporation Park Department. Former councillor –'

Cole waved a hand. 'We can only give it a line, we can't bother now with things like that –' Suddenly he became aware of a woman's startled face behind Johnson. He forced an anguished smile. 'Sorry, madam, we'll do a big story in Monday's issue.' Monday was in eternity. He resumed reading the times.

Mechanically Cole passed on sheet after sheet of copy, racing through the short clipped copy-book sentences until his head reeled. The sound of the clattering typewriters began to grate on his nerves, so that this whole body ached besides the jabs in his stomach. He felt hot and sick. In a daze he noticed Orpington rush in, flash some pictures in front of him and dash out again. Cole picked them up, eyed them through a blur, despatched them to Stack. They were late; perhaps, everything would be late ... I shall be late, he thought oddly, and knew he would have to spend the Sunday in bed.

The door opened. In it, framed regally and handsomely, still in his overcoat, stood Rankin. He strolled over to Cole's desk and regarded him accusingly.

'Really, Cole, I asked specially for those galleys ...'

Cole grimaced. 'Sorry – I – there's a boy here waiting ...' He shouted at the boy to collect a set of galleys from Mr Stack. 'I'll send him up to you at once,' he added, half hoping that Rankin would retire out of harm's way.

'All right,' said Rankin grudgingly, but he showed no signs of going. Instead he sauntered over to the overcrowded telephone booths and peered genteelly over Groves' shoulders. A moment later he beckoned Cole urgently.

'I say, Cole, keep your eyes open – there are already four spelling mistakes in eight lines.' A podgy, reprimanding finger poked into Groves' arm. The reporter looked up startled, a little frightened, and nodded dumbly.

Rankin moved on to the next booth. Cole watched, feeling his limbs begin to shake. He could not mouth the words of excuse that had risen hotly.

Rankin suddenly tut-tutted. An actual look of distress passed over his usually calm face.

'This man must be a fol. He's leaving out words. Look!'

With someone else Cole might have instinctively felt the underdog's sympathy, seeing it was Rankin's accusation. But looking at Atkinson's troubled, bowed head he saw only an object upon which to concentrate his pent-up resentment. Bending forward he saw that here and there were gaps in the lines. He shook Atkinson roughly.

Looking up, rather white-faced, Atkinson pushed the receiver phones to one side.

'I'm sorry Mr Cole. I – I – can't catch some of the words ... I've tried to get them repeated ... I don't seem to hear properly ...'

'Fool! Bloody fool!' raved Cole. 'You're letting the whole paper down ... All this time and money and trouble, and you can't take down a simple report on the phone ... Here, come away!' With a quick decisive movement he yanked Atkinson out of the seat and inserted his own thin body. He dragged the receivers on to his ears.

'Waring? ... This is Cole. Now get going.' Slowly, but with increasing speed, he began taking down the story. For the first time he felt a sense of relief. At least Waring knew something about his job; at least he, Cole knew *his* job. Now things wouldn't be botched up by thoughtless, carefree youth.

Suddenly, behind him, he sensed a commotion. Swivelling round he saw Atkinson slumped over his desk, weeping hysterically. Why, he thought, the bloody baby. As he stared, Rankin, looking a trifle nervous, started patting the heaving shoulder. Cole could almost hear him saying: 'There, there, take things easy, now ... Mr Cole didn't mean to be quite so violent ...'

Then Cole was plunged back into the whirlpool: Waring's endless, grating monotone, the bullet stutter of the rattling keys, the hot air buzzing around him, the wet, clamping, sweatiness of his body ... Waring was almost at the end, must see it through, then they wouldn't be late, then the machines would run out dry and clean and unchecked ... Now, again, under his feet, the world trembled with the rumbling presses ... There was no time to think, no time to hesitate, no time for life, only to meet the inexorable demands. Out of the corner of his eye he saw Stack, eyeing him sourly; and Rankin, worried, fussing, ready to vent his distress; and others behind them, they were all waiting, Cole sensed, waiting for the end, no doubt half hoping that the special would be late because they knew it would be his calvary. But it wouldn't, he daren't let it be, he thought. And somehow, almost ferociously, he paced Waring until, almost like a miracle, the tired voice at the other end said flatly: That's all.

The last sheet whisked off to catch the fudge. For some time they stood immobile, listening to the hum of the machines going on and on, rising up and up to the final peaks. At last, abruptly, the noise died down. A heavy silence hung over the whole building, like a passing shadow. Then, with crackling voices, the first of the red delivery vans emerged from the bowels of the Post building, racing against time and (as they secretly dreaded) the yellow vans of the *Utherton Evening News.* 'Look!' exclaimed Cole triumphantly, staring out of the window. Then – 'Oh!' he said, as a bright yellow van nosed out of the far corner of the square. Well, anyway, we weren't beaten, he thought ...

The office slowly disintegrated. Rankin cleared his throat. 'I must say,' he said severely, 'the organisation seemed to me rather haphazard. Another time I think perhaps I'd better take charge, just to be on the safe side ...'

Ah, well, all in the day's work, thought Stack placidly, going with even, unhurried steps to meet his wife outside the picture house.

Oh, dear, thought Groves, feeling rather sick, I couldn't go through that again, I don't call that being a reporter.

I can't possibly go away for the week-end, missed the last train, thought Rawlinson sadly.

He'll have come and gone by now, damn, damn, damn, thought Bromley, about his brother-in-law. And they'll have had a fine tea and chinwag.

It's not fair, not fair, thought Atkinson, staring with red-rimmed eyes at the keys of his typewriter, feeling sick and sore at heart, and much older.

Tired, overstrung, sour-faced, longing only for the peace and escape of bed, the hundred and twenty-eight staff of the

Utherton Evening Post wended a late and weary way home, jostling among the Saturday night amusement seekers. Last to leave, feeling perhaps weariest and most sick of all, Cole stopped on the way out to pick up a spare copy of the special edition. Sitting in a trolley-bus on his way home he opened out the paper tenderly. There it was ... his duty was done. The big story stretched dramatically across the whole of the front page, thick blaring headlines, several pictures, columns and columns of Waring's masterly narrative – overlapping on to the inside pages, the back page. Everything was there, down to the last gesture – a fudge of twenty lines jammed at the foot of the stop-press column.

And, straining his eyes in the dim, shaded light, Cole was just able to make out the shattering finale of the day's big story: League Cuptie – Utherton United 4 goals, Liverpool 0.

XVIII

The Three of Us

It was towards the end of one golden summer in Cornwall that
we met Mac. He came down to spend a cheap holiday, like
myself, working part-time in one of the holiday cafes and
spending the rest of the time sun-bathing on the beaches. He
was a tall, sandy-haired, soft-spoken Scotsman, not especially
good-looking, you might say, but so much alive you could not
help being drawn to him. He was a poet of sorts – what sort I
couldn't really tell you, even now. All I know is that he had a
wonderful way, specially if there was a glass of whisky in his
hand, of turning a chair round and sitting astride it, and
holding up one finger for 'Hush!' and then launching into a
string of delightful poetic fancies. I suppose they were his own:
somehow it didn't seem to matter.

Nell and I were both enchanted with Mac. Nell's my wife – or
was, that is. She had long dark hair and glowing brown eyes set
in a delicately coloured face, with high cheek bones and rich,
red, generous lips. Generous was the sort of word you used
about Nell – she had a warm nature, she gave herself ardently
to whatever interested her. There was nothing mean or small
about Nell, I can see all that.

Well, as I was saying, the three of us came together; we
became a sort of enchanted trio. Wherever we went, whatever
we did, there was a touch of magic about, Mac's magic,
perhaps. Or maybe just a communal magic, as if the three of
us, together, lit up a flame. There was Mac, with his wild Scots
ways and his halarious clowning. There was Nell, with her
radiant life and her deep, glowing beauty, with her infectious
way of opening her arms wide to the world's embrace.

And there was myself. Difficult to look in the mirror
dispassionately, isn't it? Especially when you've grown to

dislike what you see there. But at that time – well, maybe, I didn't look so closely. I know that outwardly I had what is termed 'a pleasing personality'. I was relatively intelligent and had certain talents. All this I knew because of the way Mac behaved towards me. He was younger than I, and it was indeed flattering to realize that he had a genuine respect for me – rather like that, say, of a young brother for an older one.

And then he was fond of us both, as a unit. Why, sometimes he used to tease us about it – the lovebirds he would call us. And we were, too, hopelessly in love. And Mac loved us both. That's how it was, with the months and even the years going by. We went back to London, and Mac was around there too. I was working on a newspaper by then, and Mac did some writing, too. And all the time the three of us went around together. Sometimes Mac brought a girl along, but generally he seemed to prefer being with Nell and me. It didn't seem strange, not then.

Once we did a crazy thing; went down to Brightlingsea and hired a yacht for the week-end.

On Sunday I had a bilious attack, so Mac and Nell went off, as light-hearted as ever. But when they returned later in the day they seemed subdued. Apparently the boat had got caught in a squall and capsized and they had had to cling on for half an hour before being picked up.

'Why, you idiots,' I exclaimed. 'You might have been drowned.'

Mac looked at me oddly, soberly. 'Aye, that we might.'

And he didn't say anything more for quite a while. Neither did Nell.

Soon after that my newspaper sent me on a story to Paris. Nell came with me, and we had a wonderful time. Only we missed Mac. We tried to persuade him to come, but he wouldn't. Suddenly in some odd way, he seemed the older one. It was almost as if he said, in a fatherly way: 'You run along and enjoy yourselves. Two's company, three's not – not really.'

If I'd had any sense at all, I would have left it at that. Mac had the sense all right. But I kept on at him to accompany us here and there, and in the end I usually managed to persuade him.

That was how he came with us on the trip to Cornwall. The paper wanted some silly-season stories – Cornish pixies, art colonies, ghosts and ghoulies and so on. It was a wonderful break. We lounged on golden sands, swam in clear, greeny-eyed seas, drank in a pub by the water's edge at St Ives. In a curious way the three of us seemed closer than ever.

And then there came an extra magical night, plenty of cheerful company in the pubs, a full moon over Mount's Bay and the gaiety of a dance held on the fish market at Newlyn, right on top of that lovely harbour and beside the rows of fishing boats. A lot of us piling in together and dancing ... and then, suddenly, both Nell and Mac seemed lost, swallowed among the dancers.

It wasn't for nearly an hour that I came across them again, dancing close together. I watched curiously; and then – only then – did I begin to realize what was wrong.

Or shall I say, what I thought was wrong? Nothing is quite what it seems – as Nell tried to explain later that night, when we talked things out. Now I know what she meant; then, I was too upset and alarmed to try to understand. I only knew that something was going on between my wife and my best friend, and I said so, angrily.

'It's not like that,' said Nell. 'Not the way you put it. It's partly your fault. It was all right until that day at Brightlingsea, when Mac and I were nearly drowned. We both knew then how much we cared about each other. But I loved you, too, don't you see? And so did Mac. That's why he tried to stop seeing us – only you were so stupid, you wouldn't leave well enough alone. And now ...'

I looked at her, and she shrugged helplessly.

Perhaps that was where I made my first mistake. In the morning, after a restless night, I made Nell pack her things and we drove off even before breakfast. She was very quiet, but she made no protest. By the time we were back in London, she seemed to think I had done the best thing.

In many ways it seemed I had. We resumed our life, but minus Mac. He, as a matter of fact, stayed down in Cornwall. I suppose that was his gesture, his effort to help us save ourselves. We went on living and time went by, and perhaps gradually we would have got over things. The trouble was, I could never feel sure. And there I made my second and worst mistake. I suggested next summer that for our holidays we go on a motoring tour in our new car; and I arranged that our route should take us, fairly casually, through the West Country to Cornwall – and to St Ives, where I knew we would run into Mac. I wanted to make sure that Nell didn't love him any more.

When we did meet in a pub, we weren't the same people, not really. That's life – people are altering all the time. Only I was cleverer than life – I was fool enough to think. I decided after half an hour's friendly reunion, that I can see now was quite innocent, that we were back where we had left off. The three of us were standing in a pub, as we had so often stood before, and this fair-haired man opposite was in love with my wife, and she with him. I stood in danger of losing the whole meaning of my life …

How much did I believe it? Did I really believe, or did I simply *want* to believe it? How can I say? I only know that I never even stopped to consider that perhaps Nell and Mac no longer felt the same, even saw each other in a different light. I just seethed with all sorts of long-buried resentments and fears.

When we came out at closing, I suppose we were all a bit merry, though not drunk. It was agreed we should follow Mac along the coast road to his cottage, a few miles out of town. We went to the car park, and there waiting were two cars that somehow symbolized the development of our lives – ours a brand-new, glistening, expensive sedan – Mac's a rather pathetic, old open tourer, veteran brand, with the door handle tied with string.

I can remember standing there, thinking this; and how Mac looked from one car to the other, and then at me, and knew what I was thinking. Maybe in that moment there was a sort of momentary hatred between us, even on Mac's part. He would have been only human to have felt that, as he watched the woman he loved turn and get into my car – my swanking new car.

And then I made my third, and, alas, fatal mistake. I was not big enough, generous enough, not even intelligent enough, to let it go at that. I suppose there's only one explanation: I was too much a coward at heart, and the coward always loses.

Mac started his old crock and drove off, and dutifully we followed. As we drove through the winding streets and out along the coast hill, I remembered other times we'd been driving together. I remember how both of us loved driving, and what fun we'd had in those old, carefree days, when we both gloried in having old and eccentric cars.

We drove up, out among the moors and high hills, the road winding, narrow and treacherous ...

And then, as I dutifully dawdled our new car behind the smoky one in front, I remembered something else. I remembered one of Mac's few weaknesses, something perhaps to do with his being a Scotsman – he couldn't stand being beaten at a game or competition.

I remembered how important it used to be to him to win, when, in the old days, we used to race each other in our roaring old cars. And how I always used to let him win, too – because, I suppose, I loved him.

It was in that moment that, angrily, bitterly – perhaps, who knows, malevolently? – I pressed my foot hard down on the accelerator so that our new gleaming car shot forward up the moorland road forward and outward, smoothly gliding past the little tourer and leaving it almost standing still.

I was conscious of Nell looking at me curiously. Perhaps I even guessed at the vague apprehension colouring her lovely eyes. I didn't care. I was thinking only about the man behind me. I knew Mac so well. I knew just how he would feel as the superior new car went past him – as Nell and I swept proudly ahead. I could guess at all the feelings of bitterness and impotence and anger that would crowd into him. And, wickedly, I kept my foot down on the accelerator, because I knew that Mac, being Mac, would be unable to resist tearing after us, as fast as his throbbing old crock would go.

We raced on, along that winding dangerous coastal road. I felt Nell tensing beside me. I felt the tumult of uncertain emotions rising up in her.

And perhaps indeed they did, just as, perhaps, those unworthy emotions rose up in myself, as I imagined her feeling sorry for the defeated Mac, beginning to hate the victorious me – as I drove on even faster, defying them both.

It was then we approached the hairpin bend. I remembered it from the old days. Just before we came to it, I slowed down a bit. And I could not resist looking quickly at the woman, my wife, sitting beside me.

I wonder just what was in that look? I can't be sure, even now. But I do remember the look in Nell's eyes, caught in the faint light from the car instruments. It was the startled, horrified look of one who has seen something strange and unfamiliar, like a ghost ...

The next second I turned and very deliberately accelerated the car towards the bend. I knew just what I was doing, for she was a strong and powerfully built car, with superb brakes; and, as I expected, I was able to get round that hairpin bend and shoot away down the straight.

But Mac didn't. Whether he was a bit drunk, whether he was mad with rage, or whether he was just careless – who can tell?

And after all, does it really matter? Mac and his car roared into that bend, half skidded, and then hurtled through the wooden fencing and crashed over a hundred-foot drop. When some time later, we finally found his body on the rocks below, he was quite horribly dead.

And from that moment onward, Nell believed that I had killed him. She believed that I intended the crash to happen when she caught my glance a few seconds previously. She believed that even more when we stood beside Mac's body in the light of the burning wreckage and looked, deep and desolate, into each other's eyes.

Nell left me the next day. I've never seen her since – except in my dreams. Night and day they come upon me, those dreams. Of the days that used to be. But of other things too. Of the man I once loved, of my best friend whose friendship, I repaid with – death. For didn't *I* kill Mac, really?

Oh, yes, I know that not every murderer is brought to justice. But somehow I fancy they carry their own punishment with them for a long time ... perhaps all their life.